ELLE HARTFORD

How to Treat Talking Beasts

Marine Magic #2

First published by Phoenix & Kelpie Press 2025

First edition

ISBN: 979-8-9921588-5-4

This book was professionally typeset on Reedsy.
Find out more at reedsy.com

*The greatest danger to our planet
is the belief that someone else will save it.*

~Robert Swan

Contents

Seaside
N
W
E
S
Rise estate
post office
to Inkdrop pond
lifeguard club house
boardwalk
schoolhouse
Beachy Bakes
town hall
old pier & bait shop
fishing pier & breakwater
bookstore
marina & fish market
to Zoo & Last Stop
Fisher's Village

Crew of Returning Characters

Arietta Aliona: gnome, pale wrinkly skin, light blue eyes, tuft of blue hair. Two and a half feet tall at most, she runs Beachy Bakes and has taken on *Sunlit* as a mentee; sometimes looks after *Fish.*

Biscuit Haven: New West Key Azure parrot. No one's sure how well he knows what he says. Lives in *Marine Sanctuary,* looks after *Sunlit.*

Chip Daleson: wolfkin, white hair and tail, deeply tanned, solidly built. His early morning fishing work leaves him plenty of time for ~~meddling~~ visiting friends. Son of *Pa,* adoptive father of *Fish,* partner of *Ige,* best friend to *Sunlit.*

Fish Daleson: extremely rare example of a pelagic (deep sea) merfolk child, though no one in Seaside knows this; they know only that he showed up last spring alone, and can manipulate water. Skin ranges from gray to blue, no hair, blue eyes, flat nose, gills. Adores *Sunlit, Chip, Ige, Joy, Pa,* and sometimes *Biscuit.*

Ige Afolayan: merfolk, of the Afolayan clan which has settled outside Seaside. Dark skin, shaved head, blue-purple scaled legs and large purple eyes. Chooses to live on land and takes his job as lifeguard very seriously. Brother of *Taiwo,* partner of *Chip,* and dear friend of *Fish* and *Sunlit.*

Joy: giant otter; can talk, and will cheerfully share her opinions. Arrived in Seaside during a storm and her injuries necessitated

Sunlit's arrival. Now helps run *Marine Sanctuary* and looks after *Sunlit* and *Fish*.

Marine Sanctuary: an old bait shop, saved from demolition and converted into a marine animal rescue by *Sunlit*, with the aid of all her friends.

Officer Ebb: Authoritative and steady, has been chief of police for Seaside for decades. Coastal elf with sandy skin and graying hair, steely blue eyes. Kindly toward newcomers *Sunlit* and *Fish*, frequent collaborator with *Taiwo*.

Pa Daleson: wolfkin, white hair and tail, dark eyes. Retired from fishing due to an injury to his back, and has devoted his free time to carpentry. Dotes on *Fish*, often aids *Sunlit* and *Joy*, and lovingly puts up with his exuberant son *Chip*.

Rachel Patel: catkin, with catlike ears and tawny skin, hair cut short and dyed violet, golden eyes. An official scholar, she inherited the local bookshop from her cousin and runs the town archive; wears black scholarly robes accented with colorful glasses. Friend to *Marine Sanctuary*, and considered awfully cute by *Sunlit*.

Sunlit Haven: appears human, though perhaps with a little magic (nonverbal communication with animals) and a little curse (extremely sun-sensitive skin). Pale yellow skin, pastel pink hair, light eyes. Often anxious outside of her work but excellent with animals. Moved to Seaside from New West Key. Runs *Marine Sanctuary* with *Joy*, temporarily housed *Fish*, and is responsible for *Biscuit*.

Taiwo Afolayan Rise: merfolk, prefers they/them pronouns. Dark skin, bright purple eyes, long braided black hair and purple scales. Enthusiastic and charismatic representative of town council. Brother of *Ige,* patron of *Sunlit* and *Marine Sanctuary.*

Prologue

There were very few times that Spot regretted the fact that he was a cat. Almost never, in fact. But one such rare occasion struck in the office of Seaside Zoo and Aquarium as the early summer heat settled along the wooden floorboards and happy children's voices could be heard through the window. It should have been idyllic. But Spot's mood was far from cooperative.

"Salt water!" he ranted. "Magical evaluation! Wave action! The only pool we have big enough for waves is the polar bear habitat, and of course that's far too cold!"

"There's the tidal exhibit," said his assistant, with the reasonableness of someone who isn't responsible for making any final decisions.

From his perch atop the lone desk in the room, Spot flicked a look of disdain at the young man. "The tidal exhibit is three feet deep *at best.* They'd be crowding the anemones half the time!"

"Or dashed against the rocks," the assistant agreed thoughtfully.

"We're just not set up for this kind of thing," Spot continued. "It's not what we do."

"So I gathered," said the assistant, "from the committee meeting over the past hour."

His tail twitching, Spot chose to ignore this comment. The meeting had been highly unsatisfactory. None of the select group that ran the zoo had anything to suggest. And that was no ideas from a group of five talking, magical animals, mind you—really the only people who could be relied upon to have a worthwhile opinion, to Spot's way of thinking. Human assistants surely didn't count. That's why he hadn't bothered to dismiss his yet. It simply wasn't worth the effort.

"If I was *bigger*," Spot lamented, rubbing one white-tipped paw over his ear. The rest of his fur was a luxurious orange, normally groomed to perfection, but now clumps here and there were sticking up out of place. "If I didn't hate water— and didn't love sleep—if I was capable of *building* a pool—it's not that I don't wish we could help them. But the fact remains. This is *not* the kind of thing we're set up to do! We run a zoo that happens to have an aquarium, not a water theme park with a wave pool!"

"Probably too many people at those anyway," commented the hapless assistant. This seemed to give him an idea. "Have you tried asking them?"

Spot's tail now lashed with impatience. "Asking *who*?"

"You know. People."

"It's *people* who dropped them off here to begin with," Spot pointed out.

"Oh, well, naturally. But I mean *other* people, don't you know."

At this point the assistant—whose name, incidentally, was Mouse—leaned back in his rickety wicker chair and began practicing his juggling with four colorful scarves pulled from a hidden pocket. Spot's yellow eyes were drawn to the movement. His first scathing reply about *people* in general died on his whiskered lips.

"Other people," he said slowly, as though Mouse had suggested contacting aliens and Spot wanted to be sure he'd heard him right.

"Who might have pools," Mouse elaborated.

"A mere backyard wading pool will not suffice," said Spot, in his best haughty voice. The floating scarves calmed his nerves. In fact, now that he wasn't quite so upset, he seemed to remember something . . .

"Obviously it'd have to be someone with a big pool," Mouse conceded, meanwhile.

"Hush," said Spot. He was thinking. His claws dug into the desk beneath him. "There might be something . . . just up the coast, in Seaside. Do you remember reading the news about their new hospital, right on the beach? Marine something, or something Sanctuary, wasn't it?"

"Can't recall," Mouse said cheerfully. "Might have been before I started?"

"It wasn't," said Spot with a sigh. "Come on. If *you* won't be helpful, maybe Geoff will."

1

A Tidy Ship

It has been said that cleanliness is next to godliness. Unless you know a deity who's willing to take over your cleaning for you, you'll have to do it yourself, and see that your team is properly trained as well. Every animal regardless of size, type, and ability deserves a clean berth . . .

—*from* Standard Practices for a Safe & Sanitary Animal Medic

Sunlit Haven scrubbed the boards of the old shipwreck as though her life depended on it. It didn't. But little marine creatures' lives might, and to Sunlit, that was even more important.

She and her crew of one were spending the summer afternoon cleaning out their "annex:" the wreck of an old fishing boat, submerged just beneath the waves and wedged between an ancient pier and a high breakwater, conveniently positioned right behind their headquarters. Sunlit insisted upon a very regular and rigorous regimen of cleaning all areas she managed; in fact, hung on the wall over the sink in the main building (which had once been a bait shop) was a meticulous calendar of chores, crammed onto whatever wall space wasn't covered in tidal maps. There were daily chores, and weekly chores, and seasonal chores, and chores that happened whenever anyone came in dripping a great deal of oil or muck or bodily fluid. Such was life at Marine Sanctuary.

But Sunlit did not think of them as chores. Her personal tendencies toward caretaking and people-pleasing had been exacerbated by years spent at a far-off university studying marine biology and veterinary practices.

Joy, on the other hand—well, that was another matter.

The giant otter lifted her head out of the water that covered the far end of the boat's deck. For a moment she paused, special-made brush dangling from her jaws. A friend who was handy with carpenter's tools and insisted everyone call him "Pa" had crafted a sturdy handle for her so that she could more easily fulfill her role as Sunlit's assistant. But now she spat the handle out and asked, "Are we done yet?"

Sunlit hid her smile—an easy feat when wearing a positively enormous sun hat. Working with a talking, rational otter the size of a hippopotamus had plus sides: the fact that she could scrub the entire deck of a boat in an afternoon using a custom brush, for example. But it also had downsides. Like a certain lack of attention span and a predilection for telling people exactly what they smelled like, good or bad.

"I'm not done yet," Sunlit replied diplomatically.

"Maybe you should be. Just for a moment."

Sunlit hesitated. Her shoulders ached, her fingertips were pruney, and her waterlogged pants clung to her legs uncomfortably. It was a very still, very hot day, and the fumes from her cleaning potion were starting to make her a little dizzy, now that she paused long enough to notice. Though naturally pale yellow, her skin was looking unnaturally wan. She had to admit that maybe, just maybe, Joy's refusal to work herself—or anyone else—utterly to the bone *wasn't* a downside. "A break might not be a bad idea . . . I wanted to be done before Fish gets here after school, but . . ."

"I'm sure Fish would rather watch you work—or help you work—than have to scrape you off the boat you just cleaned because you collapsed from heat exhaustion," Joy declared. "I'll get the iced tea and sandwiches."

Sunlit knew from experience not to argue.

She hauled herself up onto the nearby pier, letting her feet dangle over its side. As she sat there, the bottoms of her boots skimmed the water which filled the old boat's hull. Though the pier was perfectly dry, her head swam. She was, she realized, rather tired.

And at the same time, Sunlit Haven was struck by a quiet moment of pride. From her seat, she could survey not only her annex, but the Sanctuary itself, rising above on her left. At one time, the simple two-story building had been a bait shop, serving fishing boats that docked at the pier before the new marina had been built and business had, for lack of a better phrase, dried up. Now, nestled under the thatched roof was an attic apartment and a main floor with rows of tanks for smaller creatures, an exam room, and a sales counter that did a respectable business in sunscreen potions and informational pamphlets. Thanks to a visionary—and vocal—friend on town council, the Sanctuary benefited from government support, which covered everything that the sunscreen and medicine sales did not.

Sunlit continued considering her workplace and home. The sun was just barely beginning to sink over the water, and by tilting her head in a landward direction, she could get the brim of her hat to completely cover her shoulders. Her hair, pastel pink and cut into a short pixie cut, wouldn't shade her: in fact, it was—as usual—stuffed entirely under the hat, unhelpful. Not that her long sleeved top was slipping, of course, but the added shelter from the sun was nice.

Like Sunlit's needs, the needs of the Sanctuary were simple. Its primary expense was the plethora of fish with which Sunlit "paid" Joy, which were supplied at alarmingly low cost by yet more friends with a thriving fishing business run out of the nearby marina. The fishers insisted that because Sunlit and Joy took all their odds and ends and bycatch, they were actually doing the fishing boats a favor, and that therefore the low price was justified. Sunlit wasn't entirely sure about that, but she didn't want to push it. She liked having a budget that balanced at the end of the day, if only barely.

This same attitude of benign, if bemused, gratitude was one Sunlit applied to having so many friends in general. She had worked with many students at university, of course, and had lived with and taken care of extended family members most her life, but she had never before had so many *friends*. Sometimes the customs of community life confused her a great deal. However, if she ever tried to withdraw or isolate herself without good cause, she was sure to get a talking-to from Joy. So she'd had to accept her new circumstance . . . and in consequence, she thought as she looked up at Marine Sanctuary, they'd been able to rescue and rehabilitate so many marine creatures over the past year. Surely that was a very good thing.

Joy's whiskered nose poked out of the Sanctuary's back door. In the next moment, the otter wound her way sinuously down the rope ladder into the annex and then along the edge of the pier to Sunlit. She moved with grace and speed—her front paws distinctly *not* carrying any sandwiches or tea.

"Now, kit," she said quickly, using the otter term for children, "promise me you won't get upset."

"Why would I?" Sunlit asked, puzzled.

"Promise me you'll be calm and think about it," Joy insisted.

"About what?" asked Sunlit. She hoped she'd never given Joy the impression she would get angry over sandwiches.

"I told them to come round the side," Joy said inscrutably.

Sunlit's gaze drifted over Joy's furry shoulder—and for a moment, her heart *did* stop. Two figures were emerging from the Sanctuary's side door, which let out onto the pier (a much safer route for visitors than Joy's preferred obstacle-course of ladders and boat railings). The first, Sunlit could recognize even at a distance. It was Rachel, the local bookseller—petite, with cat ears and violet hair cropped short, and almond-shaped eyes and very cute glasses and—

With an effort, Sunlit refocused herself. It wasn't odd for Rachel to drop by; it was her printing expertise that had guided them in making the Sanctuary's information pamphlets, after all. Why did Joy think that seeing Rachel would make Sunlit upset? A flush rose on Sunlit's cheeks.

But then their second visitor caught her attention. At first, their shape was difficult to make sense of: a large, birdlike head, rising no higher than Rachel's, two lumps at the side— wings—and an unusual gait. As though they were walking on four legs instead of two. *A griffin,* Sunlit realized.

That still didn't make sense to her, though. Griffins were a very unusual sight in Seaside, to be fair, but why would meeting one be upsetting?

As the visitors approached, Sunlit scrambled to her feet. Joy slipped around her, a habitual pose, so that the otter's face was on one side of Sunlit and her body and tail were tucked neatly behind her. It was a polite way for a very long creature to make sure she wasn't blocking anyone in the conversation—and also to make sure Sunlit had someone to fall back on . . . or someone to prevent her from backing away.

"So, this is Sunlit," Rachel was saying to the griffin as they approached. Sunlit could have melted right back down onto the pier, but then Rachel turned to her. "Sunlit, this is Geoff. He's a member of the executive board that runs Seaside Zoo and Aquarium."

Executive? Rather than melting, now Sunlit was shrinking. The griffin seemed to be scrutinizing her—though perhaps a creature with the head of a bird of prey always had a scrutinizing sort of expression. Still, between his attention and Rachel's, Sunlit had never felt so self-conscious of her appearance—her posture rounded from hours of leaning over, her frame hardly slender or elegant; not to mention her sturdy, unfashionable clothing, which was hardly presentable when water-logged and splotched with cleaning potions.

"Geoff came to the bookstore just now," Rachel went on, "hoping that I could tell him where to find you. It seems funny, doesn't it, that you've been here just over a year now and yet you two have never met?"

"Is it?" Sunlit asked faintly, fixing wide, pale eyes on the griffin. "I'm sorry, um—Geoff. I don't get out much, I guess."

"Miss Sunlit Haven," Geoff began, in a scratchy and rather formal voice. The pristine feathers of his head and neck were brilliantly white in the sunlight, forcing Sunlit to squint at him as he spoke. "I'm here on behalf of the entire board of the Seaside Zoo. We're very sorry we haven't reached out to you sooner. We were, of course, delighted to learn about your venture and your mission here in town."

"Uh . . . thanks," Sunlit said. She'd never heard of this zoo before, and she was struck suddenly with a terrible feeling of impostor syndrome. Had she been stealing business from them somehow? Crowding in on their territory? Why had it never come up? Even though Geoff was saying nice things so far, his tone definitely held a note of "worse things to come."

"He said in the shop they might want to collaborate on something," Joy said helpfully.

Sunlit's alarmed gaze slid to Rachel, who shrugged. Apparently, Geoff hadn't told anyone else the details of *why* he wanted to find Marine Sanctuary.

Geoff coughed, his beak tucked behind one white wing for a moment, as though he was embarrassed. His clawed front feet scratched at the boards beneath him. "Collaborate . . . yes. Maybe that wasn't quite the right word."

Sunlit could feel her breath coming short. What was it Joy had said? *Be calm and think about it.* What if he was going to tell her to stop taking in animals? What if he wanted Marine Sanctuary to shut down?

"There's been a little trouble at Last Stop, and . . . The fact of the matter is, we have a request to make of you," Geoff said squarely.

Sunlit looked instinctively to Joy. "Last Stop?"

"It's another town, farther down the coast," Rachel put in.

"Technically Seaside Zoo is closer to them, and falls under their jurisdiction. Right, Geoff?"

"Correct." The griffin seemed relieved to find this new avenue of conversation. "It's not as touristy, but full of old vacation homes. It used to be the last stop on the commuter rail from Brass, you see."

Sunlit nodded politely, bewildered.

"Yes," Geoff continued, as though in conversation with himself, "well, in the past year or two, they've been having a bit of a renaissance there, I understand. Fixing things up, more town events, you know how these things go. The trouble is, a few days ago—the Opening Day of the summer season— they put on a brand new fireworks display, one they've never done before."

"Oh!" Joy perked up. "Is that what that was? We saw the lights. Very pretty."

"Pretty, yes, but," Geoff's voice lowered, "there were *casualties.*" When all three listeners startled, he nodded and went on, "The town feels terrible about it. So they say. But the fact remains that they've brought them to *us*, at the Zoo, and—well, normally we'd be pleased to take over, but with these—it's really not the kind of thing we do."

Sunlit caught a glimpse of salvation and jumped for it. "You mean you have wounded animals? And you'd like me to take a look at them?"

"Mostly we'd like you to take them," Geoff said in a rush. Glancing over his left wing at the annex submerged in the water below, he added, "Maybe you can house them in your charming . . . boat?"

2

A Rescue Mission

Of course, you may well expect that the best way to get to Seaside is by sea, and there is indeed a bustling port nearby. But most tourists are coming from further inland to get to the shore. The train was once a popular choice, but if you get the chance, don't hesitate to travel by air. The view of the beach and nearby jungles from a balloon or magical vessel is simply incredible.

—from A Guide to Seaside (for the Discerning Tourist)

At this point, in Sunlit's mind, the scene should have cut away to her meeting the animals in need. And while that would have been a very gratifying transition, the fact remained that Seaside Zoo was not actually *in* Seaside. Geoff had flown into town, of course; he soon took his leave and flew back to the zoo, promising to arrange everything there. That left Sunlit with some organization to do.

First, she ran inside to hastily throw some first aid items into the nearest bag. Joy followed, and opted to stay at the shop. She often took her afternoon nap behind the counter, and someone had to be on hand for Fish's arrival, just in case. Rachel, however, seemed very invested in this new adventure. She didn't offer to leave, and Sunlit was happy not to bring the matter up.

Nevertheless, transportation was still a problem. As a rule, in Seaside people either walked or swam or sailed. There was a ferry and, indeed, an old train, but those lines were not entirely helpful. There were bikes, too, but those were mostly for the tourists. No doubt this explained partly why Sunlit had not yet ventured beyond the borders of her new home town. But now that she had a *reason* to get to Last Stop, she was determined and energetic.

And that energy did not have long to wait.

"Ahoy, there!" A voice called from the ocean. "Saw you had a new visitor. Was that a griffin?!"

"Chip!" Sunlit turned and ran down to the end of the pier at once.

"Don't think you've ever been so happy to see me," Chip told her, grinning. His warm brown eyes were often smiling, set in creases in his deeply tanned face. "Oh, hey, Rachel. What's all the excitement?"

Sunlit beamed down at him. Chip, a sailor with wolfish blood in his veins—not *werewolf*, mind you, but *wolfkin*, meaning he had white wolf ears and a fluffy tail every day of the month— bobbed up and down with the waves. He was in the little dinghy his family sometimes used for quick trips or to aid their larger fishing vessel. It was strewn about with coils of rope and flotation devices and someone's half-eaten lunch. Not quite perfect, but Sunlit decided it would do. "We need your boat!"

"And you, to drive it," Rachel added, sounding distinctly amused. "Are you doing anything?"

"I was going to meet Fish here later and—"

"Joy's waiting for him, and we'll be back soon anyway. Hopefully," Sunlit said. "Can you take us down the coast to the Seaside Zoo and Aquarium? Can you get to it from the water?"

"The old zoo? Sure, I can take you there," Chip said agreeably. "It's not *right* on the beach, so you'll still have to walk a bit, but it's a lot better than walking from here." A shout could be heard from the direction of the beach. Chip glanced past them: technically, no boats were allowed so close to the old pier and, more worryingly, the breakwater. "Come on," he urged. "Hop in, I'll take you now."

Despite his habitual lack of concern for the rules, Chip was a competent captain. The moment Rachel and Sunlit clambered down from the pier and into the little craft, he steered them away. They went out around the breakwater and past the new marina at a fast clip.

Rachel took a seat on one of the benches that lined the sides of the boat, but Sunlit couldn't be still. She stood next to Chip as he operated the boat's small magitech motor, hugging her bag in both arms. Magitech was rare in Seaside, and limited almost exclusively to powering small boats like this one; the local fishing industry as a whole seemed to have decided long ago that this was the highest purpose to which steam and magic could be put. It was true that sailors were often superstitious, and any device that seemed to run on pure luck and the occasional swift kick bordered on a jinx.

That said, as the clustered masts and colorful clapboard

homes of Seaside's fishing neighborhood faded behind them, even Sunlit noticed how well the boat was running.

"Ige," Chip said, grinning, when Rachel commented on their speed. "He and Fish've been tinkering with the engine at night. At first I figured, how much harm could they do?"

"Seems they've helped," Rachel observed.

"Made my life heaps easier," Chip agreed. "But don't tell Ige I said that. How about we see what it can really do?"

He turned a dial, and the boat roared forward. Sunlit was nearly knocked overboard by the sudden increase in speed. And this was when her timeline really did collapse, and just a few breathless moments later, the boat was beached at a quiet spot on the coast.

"Not bad," Chip said, looking fondly at the boat despite the fact that all three passengers had a wiggle in their legs as they emerged onto the safety of dry land. "I still think magitech of any kind'll scare the fish away, but for little trips—that was fun."

Sunlit shook herself straight. She wasn't here for speeding boats and fun: there was a wounded animal waiting. As she scanned the coastline, though, all she saw was a palm tree jungle rising up from the sand—and a dirt road leading inland.

Just as she was about to turn and ask Chip if he was *sure* he'd taken them to the right place, Geoff the griffin landed heavily in the sand a few steps away.

"Just saw you coming," he said, ruffling his feathers into place as he folded his large wings. "Perfect timing. And you are? And that is?"

"Call me Chip, and that's my craft, the Ige Special," Chip said with a wide smile. His short white hair had been windswept into a permanent wave back from his forehead. "Just here to help the Professor."

Geoff hesitated. "The . . .?"

"That's me," Sunlit said. She'd long ago given up fighting the nickname. The fact that she didn't have *that* kind of degree really only seemed to matter to her, not to her friends.

"Oh. Of course." Geoff began walking toward the dirt road, and as the three visitors fell into step around him, he explained. "You must forgive us for being careful. Seaside Zoo was started decades ago as a sanctuary for magical animals who had had . . . *dubious* encounters with humanoids, at best. A few of us on the board still remember those days."

"But now it's one of the biggest attractions in Last Stop," Rachel said, not so much a question as a suggestion to continue.

Geoff nodded, not without pride, as they passed into the shade of the palm trees. "Shortly after we'd founded this place, we recognized the possibility of taking in other animals. Over the years we expanded. Today, the Zoo hosts an aviary, a nocturnal house, a pond habitat, a polar area, and more. Taking on more lives meant taking on more cost, and eventually— despite misgivings—we opened our doors to the public."

Sunlit scanned the trees and blooming shrubs around them, eager to get to their destination. It wasn't that she didn't appreciate the zoo's mission . . . but there were more pressing matters on her mind than history.

Chip, however, was friendly as always. "Our field trip here when I was a kid was the highlight of school," he said. "Sorry to think we were causing anyone trouble."

"Oh, no." Geoff's voice softened. "The children rarely do. Do not mistake me—it has been good, very good, sharing our zoo with the public. We love what we do. We just can't help but cling to the old ways now and again."

"Neither Sunlit nor I grew up here," Rachel said. "I have to admit, I haven't been here yet either. It's in all my regional guidebooks though."

"In that case," Geoff said, turning off the road, "let me be the first to welcome you to the Seaside Zoo and Aquarium."

It was immediate and magnificent. Sunlit only barely registered the fact that the road had opened up onto a dirt parking lot behind them. Geoff's turn took them through a tunnel of foliage and fairy lights, which opened up onto an animal lover's dream.

It was like a fairy tale oasis. Each building was unique, themed like the exhibit it housed inside. A dark castle with spires for the nocturnal species, a towering aviary, low walls with mosaics and thatched roofs mingled among carts selling sweet snacks and sparkling lemonades. As they passed the entrance gate, a group of children ran by, each sporting charmed animal costumes—a ladybug, a gazelle, a tiny dragon.

Suddenly, Sunlit understood why Geoff had been telling them the zoo's history. This was a place that merited an introduction.

Still, though, she was there for a reason. She shouldered her bag and cleared her throat. "Which exhibit do you have the patient in?"

"That's the trouble," Geoff said, hedging. "We really don't have a deep sea exhibit. Ah . . . Here's Mouse. It's been his job to coordinate with them."

"With who?" Sunlit frowned.

Next to her, Rachel sucked in a breath. "He's kind of cute, don't you think?" she whispered.

Sunlit's frown deepened. For the first time, she focused on the stranger conferring with Geoff.

Mouse was a human, tall and thin, and yet he gave an

impression that *was* rather mouse-like at first glance. He had dark skin and brown eyes behind wire-rimmed spectacles, and thick curly black hair. He stood with a slight stoop, belying the professional air of his blue suit. In his hands he held pinwheels and a large rubber ball, as though he'd just come from a playground. Nothing about him made sense to Sunlit, especially not in this context.

"Headed for the fire, are you?" Mouse addressed their little group with a light air and an easy smile. He was easily taller than all three of them, even when one counted Chip's and Rachel's ears—and Sunlit's hat. "I'll escort you, if you don't mind, that is."

"No, we're not, I'm here to—" Sunlit planted her feet as she spoke, and Rachel, who had already started walking behind her, collided with her shoulder. They tripped over each other's feet and both went tumbling forward—until faint gold sparkles caught them by the shoulders and set them upright again.

"Flunked out of Witch school in Argen, but I can do a little," Mouse said kindly. He'd dropped his props; now he held his hands aloft, and the gold sparkles emanated from them. "You're alright, I hope?"

"Perfectly," Rachel said, coming forward. "But you've dropped all your things. Are you always such a mess?" She bent down to retrieve the scattered pinwheels and came back up smiling, teasing him.

Mouse seemed just as surprised by it as Sunlit was. But he reacted much more positively. "Occupational hazard," he told Rachel, returning her smile.

"What occupation is that?" she asked, holding the pinwheels like a bouquet.

"Depends who you ask," he returned. "Why don't you keep

those for now? They're much safer with you, I'd bet."

"I'll look after them very carefully," Rachel promised.

Sunlit was staring at them. Chip was staring speculatively at Sunlit.

Mouse turned and seemed to see both Sunlit and Chip for the first time. "Oh, sorry, don't you know. I know you're not here about a fire. It was just a little shorthand of mine. You see, they're in an old fire truck at the moment."

Sunlit was still speechless, so Chip said obligingly, "Who is?"

"Didn't you know?" Mouse smiled at them. "The porpoises."

3

A Bittersweet Fire

There are many types of porpoises in Beyond. They can be found in every large body of saltwater. Though the sizes, colors, and diets of each species vary, they are in general gregarious, seafaring mammals. Though most varieties have no inherent magic, they are favorites with whale-watching tourists, and as such may sometimes be found in danger . . .
—*from* Traverse's Guide to Marine Vertebrates, Invertebrates, and Magical Outliers

Mouse set off with a long stride, navigating the winding pathways of the zoo like an expert guide. There was no time to talk, which was exactly to Sunlit's taste. They'd wasted quite a bit of time already.

There was no time to talk—and yet there was Rachel, keeping step with Mouse, and she *was* talking to him. Her tawny ears bobbed and flicked as she laughed.

Chip nudged Sunlit, but she ignored him.

Then Mouse led them down a side path that cut behind the exhibits, and Sunlit could truly focus at last. There, hidden behind the high walls of a savanna exhibit decorated with bending grasses and sun motifs, was a dusty maintenance yard—and in the middle of it there was, indeed, an old fire truck.

Sunlit had grown up in locales more likely to mold than catch fire, and she'd never given much thought to how fires were fought. The machine in front of her was magitech, like Chip's boat motor, but its wooden cab and bed sat solidly on six rubber wheels. Behind the driver's cab there was a massive drum, big enough to safely store Chip's entire boat if need be. Though most of the truck was painted bright orange, the drum itself was metal, and the rust spots gave away what it was for. Hoses and ladders were stacked at the back, where a platform had been built up behind the drum.

"It's amazing," Sunlit said as she looked up at it. She'd momentarily forgotten everything else.

"It's something." Another new person, this one a gray-skinned elf in a police uniform, emerged from the truck's shadow. "Been rusting behind town hall for years, but it came in handy now. You Sunlit Haven?"

Sunlit tugged her sleeves down, reminded of how strange this all was. In that moment, another shape emerged from the shadow—this one familiar. Another police officer, but this one from Seaside, with a knowing look on his tan face.

"That she is," Officer Ebb told his companion. He was also an elf, but one of the native coastal variety with sand-colored skin and long sharp ears. His blue eyes, often steely, swept over the incoming party. "Looks like she brought company, too."

"But if *you're* here, then why—" Chip protested.

Officer Ebb shrugged. "Emme here got hold of me not long ago. Maybe you folks and I crossed paths on the way here."

"I got tired of waiting," Officer Emme explained. She was rather stocky for an elf, and the tight braid in her dark hair revealed she was missing part of one ear, but it was her light eyes and laid-back tone that really struck Sunlit. "I didn't realize the zoo had already reached out to someone. Someone has to stay with the truck, but I do have other things to do."

"And they shouldn't stay in there," Sunlit said, looking up again. "If that's really where they are? In that drum? Can I climb up?"

She was already on her way to the back of the truck. As she went, she caught Officer Ebb give Officer Emme a meaningful glance, but didn't try to think what it might mean. She left the others talking as she hoisted herself up onto the bed of the truck and began to climb. A platform had been built level with the upper lip of the drum, but it was narrow, just big enough for her and her bag. Kneeling there with her equipment, she saw them for the first time.

Porpoises, Mouse had said. He was partly right. There was a fully grown one, easily as long as Sunlit was tall, and a baby; they were almost motionless in their pool, the adult using its head to hold the baby up so that it could breathe. By the shape and size of the adult, Sunlit knew at once that they were western bay porpoises.

But—western bay porpoises were supposed to be blue-gray on top, with white-gray bellies. These two porpoises . . .

Sunlit leaned over the platform to peer down at her companions. "What happened?"

"Magic went awry at the fireworks show." Officer Emme shielded her face with her hand as she looked up. "That's as much as I could tell you."

"Sometimes if a spell is too big, it can get away from the caster and sort of infect people," Mouse added, clearly doing his utmost to be helpful.

Sunlit retreated to consider the porpoises once more.

The adult's skin was patterned in hues of green, like it had been dip-dyed—or scorched. The darkest green patch was on the side of its head nearest Sunlit, while the lightest shades seemed to be streaked along its tail. Shivers of color ran over the baby's skin, changing it from purple to pink to yellow to blue in an erratic, unending display. While she watched, the adult shifted, bobbing its head down to let the baby go. Freed of its duty for just a moment, the adult broke the surface of the water and took a deep breath. But the baby—Sunlit bit her lip. The baby didn't swim. Instead it slowly bobbed lower in the water until the adult lifted it up again.

She knew as much as she could figure out from a distance. Reaching into her bag, she pulled out a sealed container of fish and took off the lid. The moment she lowered the fish into the water, she had the adult porpoise's attention.

Much like the leaders of the zoo, the porpoise was cautious. But Sunlit was patient. She waited, and as she waited, she spoke to the porpoise very quietly. "It's alright, friend. I'm only here to help. I want to know what happened. But I can't tell how to make things better from here. If you come over, I can help. You can have this fish, too. I have more. Is that your baby? Does your baby need food, too?"

The porpoise moved in her direction, slowly. It wouldn't lift its head out of the water—Sunlit saw that, and understood. To do so would disturb the baby. So she leaned down and held the fish deeper underwater. The porpoise took one from her, gently, and then another. As it ate, she tugged one of her gloves off very carefully. With her hands underwater, she didn't have to worry about sun exposure in the same way as in the open air. Once her hand was free, she eased her fingers along the porpoise's head.

"Sunlit?" Chip's voice came from below, concerned. "You're not touching it, are you? Tell me you're not."

"I have to, Chip," Sunlit said without moving.

"It's probably fine," Mouse put in. "The magic probably wouldn't spread any more . . ."

Below, they fell to discussing magical mishaps. Rachel was explaining a great deal of theory. Rachel was so smart, and yet Mouse . . .

Sunlit shook her head and focused. If she was still, and open, she could often get a feeling from her animal charges. It wasn't magic or divination—it wasn't anything Sunlit had ever been able to explain. But it was a little spark of confidence, of knowing. That was what she needed now.

It came in a wave from the adult porpoise. It was male—his name was Zila. Zila's feelings of anxiety, sadness, and confusion felt familiar to Sunlit.

"I know it's hard right now," she whispered. "But are you hurt?"

Zila twisted away from her, swimming in a small circle around the drum, pushing the baby along with him. As he paused again to breathe, going through the same motions as before, Sunlit understood. His movements were all perfectly normal, albeit confined by his tank. When he came back, she gave him her last fish and inspected the splotch of dark green above his eye as best she could through the water. When she ran her fingers over it, he didn't flinch.

"I don't think he's in any physical pain," Sunlit said aloud, not realizing that her audience below had no idea which porpoise she meant. "I'm really not sure if the color change is permanent. There are some creams I could try. But the baby . . ."

Moving very carefully, she eased her hand up to the baby's snout, which rested just at water level. She'd been afraid to touch it. Partly because it might worry Zila, but partly because of the baby's eerie motionlessness.

"The baby is very upset." She didn't even have to touch it—just look in its eye to know that. Ignoring the color effects and just looking at its skin, she could tell that it was dehydrated from being held above water so much. Experimentally, she ran her fingertip along the baby's back, even over places where its color was changing. She did feel a little tingle of energy where the yellow switched into orange and then to blue, but other than that, nothing. Frowning, she lifted the baby's tail, then tickled its tummy. That made it twitch away from her—just a little bit.

"It can move," Sunlit said with relief. Even Zila seemed heartened, bobbing up just a little in the water. "It *is* responsive. It needs skin care and definitely some milk, and probably a lot of rest. They must have both had a terrible shock. And they seem . . ." Sunlit hesitated before saying *sad.* Remembering her varied audience, she shied away from revealing so much. She didn't like to admit to the feelings she got from animals, simply because she didn't like to try to explain something she barely understood. Instead she asked, "Were there others? This kind of porpoise usually lives in small family groups, especially at this time of year."

"There was a pod spotted this morning off the coast of Seaside, but every member seemed to be perfectly healthy," Officer Ebb reported.

"Of these ones though, there *was* one that didn't make it." Emme's voice was somber. "It was at the center of a magical explosion. Witnesses said it just disappeared."

"The mother," Sunlit realized sadly, watching Zila and his baby. "I understand."

"Can you take them?" Mouse's voice floated up, hopeful. "We'd all be bally well pleased if you could. Everyone here wants the best for them, hand to heart, but they're so much bigger than most of our aquatic pools . . ."

"Yes, I will take them," Sunlit said decisively. Her left hand twinged at her—she'd been doing too much work today already without her gloves on, even with her hands in the water. Now that the porpoises were out of reach, she could notice it. But she ignored the sensation for now. "I'll take them right now. We'll make sure that they're well."

"Of course we will," Chip agreed, unseen. "So—how will we get them home?"

4

A Small Tub

*If you have to go to Seaside, go in the spring or the fall.
Even in the winter, it's worth it. But at all costs, if you're
the kind of adventurer who likes to stay off the beaten
path, avoid Seaside in summer!*
—from I'm An Adventurer Here Myself

Sunlit found herself relieved when Mouse took his leave, running off into the zoo to inform the board members. She was saved from dwelling on this emotion, however, by an emerging back-and-forth between Last Stop's Officer Emme and Chip.

"Seaside isn't *so* out of your way, is it?" Chip was saying.

"By road, it's an hour round trip, at least," the officer retorted, "and my shift ended three minutes ago."

"Then maybe we should just borrow—"

"Have you ever driven anything on land?" Emme interrupted skeptically.

"Maybe our town lifeguards, up a tree," Officer Ebb put in with an amused look on his weathered face.

Chip was never so easily deterred. "But I'm sure it's—"

"Very complicated," Officer Emme said firmly.

"But if the porpoises are already *in* there—"

"Is all this just because you want to drive a fire truck, Chip?" Rachel asked.

"Well . . ." Chip looked around sheepishly, then up at Sunlit. "You agree with me, right? It'd be cool."

"It'd be simplest for the porpoises," she corrected, although privately she agreed with him. This ancient fire truck was the coolest thing she'd seen on land in quite a while. Aside from the Zoo itself, of course. "However, we do need to transfer them back into the sea at some point, to eventually get them into the annex back home." *Back home*—these days, Sunlit could say such a thing without even stumbling. "And the sooner they're out of this drum, the better. I'm sure it's far too warm now to be comfortable. I think Z—I mean, the adult porpoise—can swim just fine. We could guide him alongside your boat, Chip. The trouble is the baby . . . It'd be best to have him in the boat with us. I'm afraid it will upset Zila very much, but there's no way we can trust the baby in open water."

Chip scratched his head, his ears cocked much like an inquisitive canine. "The real trouble is that my boat, unlike yours, Professor, won't work very well if we fill it with water. I don't suppose your baby porpoise likes dry land?"

"Definitely not," Sunlit replied. There *were* such things as moisture spells, even towels that could be wrapped around a creature and keep it just as wet as if it was fully submerged— but such magical conveniences were expensive, and very hard to get hold of in Seaside. She made a mental note to write to

Professor Lina (an *actual* professor, and occasional benefactor of Marine Sanctuary) to see about getting some for future rescues.

In the pause, Officer Emme cleared her throat. At the same time, Rachel lifted her hand as though an idea had occurred to her. However before either could speak Mouse barreled back into their midst, carrying something that seemed to be an actual barrel.

He held it up to Sunlit with an air of triumph, and she saw that it was in fact a large, shallow tub, the kind that might once have been a water trough in an exhibit. Though she was loath to admit it, it would be the perfect thing to transport the baby porpoise in. Especially once it was full of fresh, cool ocean water.

"Spot says have it, and his compliments as well," Mouse said breathlessly. "He's in the middle of a 'Felines of the World' presentation, or he'd come here himself. Everyone's *very* excited, don't you know. Probably put up a statue in your honor or some such."

Sunlit had no idea who Spot was, and she wasn't too thrilled about this statue talk. But she chalked it up to more of Mouse's "shorthand." She'd once tutored students from Argen, and the slang of that city was faintly familiar to her ears.

As Sunlit leaned down to accept the tub, Officer Emme spoke up. "Seems to me that solves your main problem. Your boat is beached just outside the Zoo, I take it? I can drive the truck down there for you."

"Kind of you to give us the extra time," Officer Ebb told her, a twinkle in his eye. "May I ask how you got the porpoises into the drum in the first place?"

"Don't," Emme replied, momentarily closing her eyes as if

the memory was just too much. "Let's just say, the town Witch was very involved."

"If it's just a touch of magic, I can do it," Mouse offered. "I'll go with you."

Sunlit frowned down at his eager face. "Would that be safe?"

"Levitation was always my best subject, you know. That's how I caught you earlier," he said earnestly. "I could show you now—"

Golden sparkles surrounded Sunlit, and her first impulse was to yell a hasty *no, thank you!* But if she was going to trust Zila to this same spell, she had to thoroughly test it. She closed her eyes and clenched her fists as she was lifted, quite gently, from the top of the fire truck and deposited on the ground.

"You're amazing," Rachel trilled. Unfortunately, as Sunlit got her bearings, she realized Rachel was talking to Mouse.

"Oh, I was never Town Witch material, I must say," Mouse said bashfully. "But it comes in handy entertaining the kids, let me tell you."

As Officer Emme hopped into the fire truck's driver's seat and eased the contraption down a dirt road toward the beach, everyone fell into step behind it—Rachel and Mouse still enthusing about magic and spells. Sunlit walked at the back of the group, hugging her new tub and brooding. Her left hand ached. Witch school was serious business. It was much like going to university and beginning a career wrapped up in one organization: once a witch had graduated (Sunlit was unclear on the details, being thoroughly un-magical herself), they were assigned to a town, where they became an official Witch, doing things like consulting on magical problems and, apparently, lifting porpoises into fire trucks. (And perhaps endangering the porpoises in the first place? Sunlit made another mental note, this one to ask Emme who had been responsible for the loose spell.) That Mouse had flunked out—and was so blasé about it—was confusing enough to Sunlit, who had never once even considered getting a below-stellar grade in a class when she was a student. That Rachel *still* seemed to think he was the greatest thing since knights in shiny white armor was downright baffling.

Still, moving Zila into the waves went without a hitch, and that was what really mattered. Sunlit stood thigh-deep in the water, an anxious Zila beside her, as Mouse's golden magic settled the baby into the tub in Sunlit's arms. Together, the tub, water, and porpoise were very heavy. Chip waded out to help her hold it up, while Zila nudged at her hip.

"We have to, just for now," Sunlit told the porpoise. She wasn't sure exactly how much he understood; like most communal animals, porpoises were highly intuitive, but as far as she knew Zila and his family had never had contact with humans before.

"We'll have to be careful about weighing down the boat, is what we have to," Chip said.

"I'll get a ride home with Officer Ebb," Rachel volunteered from shore. "Or—?"

Even from yards away in the sea, Sunlit could see the look her friend directed at Mouse.

"Oh, gosh," said the man in question. "I'd be only too happy to help somehow, you know. We do have a sort of zoo-mobile, if you don't mind riding about with lizards and things painted on the side of the wagon."

"Not at all," Rachel laughed.

Mouse beamed. "Then your chariot awaits!"

Sunlit didn't think this was a good idea. But Officer Ebb

was avoiding her gaze, under the pretext of helping guide Emme and the firetruck back up the beach. In the end, she was outvoted.

Soon she found herself sitting on the floor of Chip's boat, one hand on the baby porpoise in a tub in front of her, Zila constantly bumping into the hand she held over the boat's side. Slowly, carefully, they were making their way back to Seaside.

The sun was starting to set over the water. When had that happened? Sunlit tugged the brim of her hat down and sat with her chin on her knees. Her left hand, normally a lemony yellow, was angry and red. What had started as the slight burn of a moment's exposure out of the water was now blisters and welts, but she couldn't let it affect her yet. Her entire life, she'd lived with the fact that her skin burned terribly when exposed to the sun. Normally she could manage it with clothes and hats, but in her haste to get the porpoises settled, she'd forgotten to put her glove back on.

All she had in her bag was first aid for animals, though, and that was disorganized at best. For now, all she decided that all she could do was hide her hand from the sun and ignore the sensation. Similarly, the baby porpoise ignored her stare.

Chip, however, had never been known to ignore anyone. From his position as pilot at the back of the boat, he couldn't see Sunlit's affliction, for which she was grateful He'd be certain to lecture her.

But he did eventually speak. His voice was sympathetic and low, just hovering over the gentle lap of the waves.

"Bit of a shock, eh?" he asked.

Sunlit refused to emerge from her huddle. "I was off-guard from the beginning. I should have asked what kind of animal it was before we left," she said. "I could have brought more fish and maybe made some milk for the baby. I've got to get better at off-site missions."

"They've only got to hold on a little while longer, and we'll be back at the Sanctuary and they can both eat as much as they like," Chip said kindly. "But that's not what I meant and you know it."

Shifting, Sunlit scanned the horizon ahead for signs of Seaside and its marina. She thought she could make out some sunset cruises and the crowd of masts in the distance, but knew that Chip would be much more familiar with where they were. There was no use arguing with him on any point, in this case.

Zila's smooth skin bumped and brushed at her fingertips as she trailed her right hand in the water. Fortunately, that hand felt fine. And Zila seemed to be swimming well, at least— though admittedly they weren't going even a fraction of the speed they'd gone earlier.

Thinking back over their whirlwind trip, and something other than her hand, Sunlit finally found words. "Chip?"

His response was immediate and pleasant. "Hm?"

"Am I—am I too focused?"

Her friend chuckled. "You sound like you've been listening to Joy."

"No, I mean it," Sunlit insisted. Something she'd often worried about in the past but always in the background now surfaced, like a certain baby porpoise held up to breathe. "Like—do I focus too much on work? Am I no fun?"

"You're adorable, Sunlit." Chip's voice was definite and reassuring. "Fish told you so just the other day, didn't he?"

She bit her lip. "That's not quite the same thing."

"No, I get it. You're right, there." Chip became thoughtful. "Everyone has their own idea of fun."

"But I'm not—" *I'm not hers,* Sunlit thought. In desperation she turned and looked over her shoulder, meeting Chip's brown eyes. Her insides felt all jumbled up. She'd really never contemplated things like *fun* and *relationships* very much before. And now that she suddenly wanted to, she found the subject extremely disheartening.

Chip seemed to understand without her saying anything more. "So don't be," he said companionably. "Be sad. It's okay, it can be rough out there sometimes. But you'll come out alright at the end."

Sunlit hesitated, then turned forward again. She wasn't sure what to say. Somehow she had a feeling that Chip was right— and at the same time, part of her didn't want him to be.

When next she was roused from her thoughts, though, she had to smile. As Chip nosed the boat up close to the pier behind Marine Sanctuary, Joy was waiting for them. And sandwiched between otter and railing was a little boy in swim trunks and a flowered shirt, waving ecstatically.

"Sunlit, Sunlit!" Fish cried. His skin today was a teal blue, his large eyes shining and the sun glinting off his bald head. "Sunlit, you're a *hero!*"

Overwhelmed, Sunlit turned back to Chip once more, for just a second. Above her smile, her eyes were swimming with unexpected tears.

"Told you," Chip said cheerfully. "Now go on and tell your porpoise friend where to go, before Ige comes and tries to give me a fine. Let's just hope the crowd on the beach slows him down!"

5

A Child's Love

> *When accepting a new animal into the hospital for a lengthy stay, it should be observed closely as it enters its new surroundings. Any problems with the enclosure are best ascertained before they become injuries or escape routes. Every effort must be made to keep the animal calm and comfortable.*
>
> *—from* Standard Practices for a Safe & Sanitary Animal Medic

"You *saved* it, Sunlit," Fish said. "Just like you saved me!"

He'd kept up this theme now for the better part of an hour. Sunlit was very familiar with Fish's enthusiasm—he was, after all, her official Junior Assistant at Marine Sanctuary. But this particular theme made her blush.

"You *saved it!*" echoed Biscuit, a brilliantly blue type of parrot known as the New West Key azure, perched on the remains of the sunken boat's mast. Normally he preferred to stay inside the Sanctuary, but all the commotion had drawn him outside. The bird was the one companion who had come with Sunlit from her previous life, and though no one could ever quite tell if he understood what he was saying, he seemed to delight in stirring up trouble. For now, Sunlit opted to ignore him.

"Technically Ige and the other lifeguards saved you, Fish," she reminded the little boy. Though truth be told, she wasn't so sure about that: Fish had turned up on the beach last summer, but he hadn't needed rescuing—he had seemed perfectly fine at the time. Since then, he'd proven himself to be almost eerily good at swimming, adept at using the gills which lined his neck—and with his own curious brand of water magic besides. Aside from the fact that he seemed to have appeared from thin air—or perhaps thin water?—there wasn't a thing wrong with him.

Fish was undoubtedly a mystery, but he was also just a child. Sunlit gently shooed his little fingers away from the baby porpoise's tub: he was tugging at the lip of it with such excitement that she feared he'd tear it apart. "And we haven't officially saved this one yet," she added, though her voice was steady. "Even though we got them both into the annex okay, we still have to feed them. Will you go see how Joy and Chip are doing with the food?"

"I'll be a marlin," Fish promised. "Did you know marlins are the fastest sea animals ever? We learned about them in school!"

"Fastest non-magical marine animals," Sunlit corrected with a small smile. "Go on then, let's see."

Fish scrambled up the rope ladder from the annex and took off at a flying sprint down the pier. Belatedly, Sunlit realized that she probably shouldn't have encouraged running on an uneven surface . . . especially one so far above the current tide. Fortunately, he didn't have far to go.

The sun had set, and though the beach was far from quiet, the waves were calm. Sunlit sat on the raised rear deck of the annex, next to the baby porpoise's tub—which was just about as tall as the water level, so the baby rested in a confined space that was still connected to the outer world as the waves rose and receded. Zila seemed to have accepted this; he rested in the deeper water just past Sunlit's knees, his unnaturally green skin blending in with the long evening shadows.

"Dinner is coming," Sunlit told him, sighing softly as she pulled off her sun hat and tossed it up onto the pier. Next she rolled up her sleeves, which had become thoroughly soaked as they settled the porpoises. Her left hand was worse than it had been in years, but she'd wrapped a handkerchief around it for now. Like Fish's heritage, this condition was a mystery. Perhaps it was hereditary, or perhaps it was a curse, Sunlit had never known which. It had certainly seemed like a curse in the beginning. Now, she was used to waterlogged clothes. But she still savored that little bit of relief each night when she could get them out of the way.

Zila whistled—whether at her or the baby, she couldn't tell. The baby was still unresponsive. Often Sunlit could at least tell what an animal's name was, and she got nothing now. She glanced up at the lit windows of Marine Sanctuary, willing Chip to work faster. He'd left to anchor his boat properly in the marina but had promised to return and help Joy prepare baby porpoise food from a recipe book in Sunlit's exam room. It was a fairly simple mix. They should be done any minute now . . .

"Who left this hat here?" A stranger peered over the railing above, looking down at Sunlit. "Is this yours?"

"Um . . . yes," Sunlit said, squinting back. She thought the person, apparently a tall and very pale lady, seemed familiar, but she couldn't place her.

"It really shouldn't be in the middle of the walkway. Someone could trip," the person said. Her tone was irritated and self-important.

Sunlit wanted to say *I only just put it there* or *I'm actually very busy with much more important things than a hat,* but she held her tongue. She was keenly aware that in that moment, she didn't look busy at all.

Besides—though she had purchased the old bait shop and the defunct pier from the city, she did not often try to restrict access to them. After all, the whole point of Marine Sanctuary was to let animals *in.* And the pier, which thanks to her friends sported a gate at the end letting out into the sea and fairy lights all along the railings, made a very attractive place to walk. It wasn't unusual for strollers from the boardwalk along the beach to add Sunlit's pier to their route.

"I'll give it back to you, shall I?" the person said, clearly expecting effusive thanks and apologies for this condescension.

"Thanks but no, actually—" Sunlit's protest was ineffective. The hat came sailing over the pier's railing. Unprepared for this turn of events, Sunlit could only watch as it arched over her and landed with a soft *thump* right on top of the baby porpoise in its tub.

Sunlit might have been stunned into silence, but Zila most certainly was not. That he had been paying very close attention to the baby's situation was immediately clear. The porpoise rose up from the annex shadows and, amid a torrent of angry clicks and whistles, spat a bellyful of water at the offending lady. It hit her square in the chest.

"What in Beyond—!" The stranger reeled, sputtering, her irritation becoming anger and then indignant rage.

Sunlit opened her mouth to say *I'm sorry,* but the words didn't come. Instead she said a bit helplessly, "He's a porpoise—they're porpoises—they need quiet and rest—they've had a very bad experience in Last Stop—they only just got here—you really shouldn't be here—"

At this the lady collected herself. "*I* shouldn't be here, you say! The *nerve!*"

"But—but—" Sunlit wavered, cursing herself roundly for not having asked Joy to close the gate to the pier.

And in that moment, Fish returned.

He was moving so fast, marlin fast. This despite the fact that he was carrying a bucket full of fish in both hands, with a bottle perched on top. Sunlit only had time to catch a glimpse of him before further catastrophe struck.

The stranger was still ranting. Fish careened right into her. Actual fish heads and tails went everywhere. The bucket itself tumbled down into the annex, which set Zila off again. The air was rife with whistles and screeches and jets of water and seafood guts.

And just then, Sunlit remembered where she'd seen this pale, prim and proper lady before.

Overcome with worry for Fish and for Zila, Sunlit's brain shut down. The lady's indignant rage had become an unearthly, passionate fury. She was yelling words like hurling lightning bolts, but it was just noise as far as Sunlit was concerned. Through the dark haze, all she could see was Fish. The little boy was desperately chasing down the contents of his bucket, despite no longer having a bucket to put them in.

"I'm sorry, Sunlit," he was saying.

"—and what the owner of a supposed Sanctuary is doing causing such mayhem—"

"I'll get all of it," Fish called to her.

"—ought to be ashamed of yourself, imagine just what the university would say if they saw this—"

"It'll be okay, we can make more," Fish added, spilling fish bits into the annex from the pier and then running to collect more.

"—dangerous animals in a public place—and you're not even paying attention!!"

"Excuse me," said a new voice, one which did not actually ask to be excused, but which demanded attention. "What's going on here?"

For the second time that day, Sunlit could have cried.

* * *

Ige Afolayan had seen many tirades during his time as head lifeguard in Seaside (and even before that, living in a merfolk settlement where tempers—including his own—occasionally ran high). It was clear he was not impressed with the tirade he witnessed now.

"You're a member of town council," he told the irate lady, once he was done listening to her shrill explanation of the situation. "You should know that this pier belongs to Marine Sanctuary. It's not unusual for hats, porpoises, or fish guts to be present here. You should also know that this kind of disturbance so near the beach doesn't reflect well on the town. If you're hurt, I suggest checking in at the lifeguard station. For anything else, go to Officer Ebb—or bring it up at your next council meeting. At the moment, it's clear that the best thing you can do is leave."

In a huffy, upturned-nose sort of silence, the lady did so. She did not so much as glance at Sunlit or even Fish, who had taken up a post glued to Ige's scaled knee.

Once she was out of earshot, Ige huffed too—a short, dismissive sigh. He ran one dark hand over Fish's smooth head. "You folks okay?"

"I was a marlin," Fish said uncertainly. "But it didn't work very well."

Sunlit broke at last. "Oh, Fish, come here," she said, letting out her own breath in one long deflation as she reached out her arms. Immediately the little boy detached from Ige and slipped down the ladder into the boat, giving Zila one wary glance. Sunlit pulled him into a tight hug. "You were perfect," she told him. "Just maybe next time we should be a little more careful."

"I know where the bottle went," Fish said, his voice muffled. "I can get it."

"Okay, good idea." Sunlit let go, only to realize that now both she and Fish smelled very strongly of—well, fish. "Wait— before you go, maybe splash some water on your shirt. It's okay, Zila's not mad at you. He's just calming down in his own way. Just stay up here on the deck with me, and you'll be fine."

The adult porpoise was, in fact, swimming tight circles within the annex's walls. But as if to prove Sunlit right, he did not so much as look at Fish while the child brushed fish tails off his clothes. And once Fish had scampered up the ladder once more, Zila scooped up a few of those fish tails from the quiet water. As he ate, his swimming slowed and the remaining tension eased.

"Figured you must have some new patients, when I saw Chip come by earlier," Ige remarked.

Sunlit sighed again, this time more naturally. "Yes, this is Zila and his baby, who doesn't seem to have a name yet. They were caught in a fireworks accident in Last Stop last night. It's been—I wish things had gone a lot smoother."

"First thing you learn in lifeguard training is to have a plan," Ige said. Then, with a rare smile, he added, "And the second thing you learn is that nothing ever goes according to plan."

As she looked up at him, Sunlit was flooded with belated gratitude. From the very start, Ige and Chip had been reliable constants in her life at Seaside. Where Chip was upbeat and kind, Ige was reserved—and kind. After a slightly misspent youth he'd grown into a safety- and rules-conscious adult, something which made him excellent at his work and highly relatable to Sunlit (not that she'd ever misspent anything, but she did like knowing the rules). His large purple eyes shone at her now through the darkness, matching the glints off the deep blue and purple scales along his calves. Merfolk were common in Seaside, but Ige was a little unusual in that he'd chosen to live on land, his tail shifted into scaled legs. Actually, Chip often said that Ige lived at work; Sunlit had only very rarely seen him *not* wearing his red lifeguard swim trunks and white button-up shirt.

"Thank you for coming over," Sunlit said. Her pier was well within view of the lifeguards' station on the beach, of course, but she wasn't used to needing help from them. "I don't even really know what happened. I—I don't know what I can say. You don't think she'll come back, do you?"

"More snail, less marlin," Ige said firmly to Fish as the boy ran past with the baby's bottle of milk in hand. Fish slowed instantly. Satisfied, Ige returned his attention to Sunlit. "I think for now, the best thing we can do is get your patients fed. Then get something to eat ourselves. Chip still around here somewhere?"

Sunlit smiled at that. "Yes, he's probably trying to help Joy clean up the Sanctuary. I do owe you all dinner. What do you say to that, Fish?"

Now at her elbow with the baby porpoise's rations, Fish beamed. "Let's get milkshakes!"

6

A Moonlit Night

The western bay porpoise will have one live calf each year or every other year, in late spring or summer. The baby relies on its mother for milk until it is approximately nine months old, though it may start eating some solid foods as early as five months.

—*from* Traverse's Guide to Marine Vertebrates, Invertebrates, and Magical Outliers

The boardwalk at Seaside was the town's main attraction— aside from the ocean, of course. One side of the wide wooden walkway opened up onto the beach, while the other side was lined with shops and games of all descriptions. If so inclined, a person could: deck themselves out in beachy silks, bob for "coconuts," spin a wheel to win a harmless spell or goofy charm, eat a cookie made to look like an oyster, blow sparkling bubbles, send a postcard, enjoy an ice cream cone, have a tropical-themed cocktail, try out guessing games or feats of strength, and even take home a new hermit crab best friend.

Sunlit was a little iffy on that hermit crab practice, but she hadn't wanted to overstep her welcome yet.

Because the truth was, most of the boardwalk's business owners and locals had been very welcoming of Sunlit and her Marine Sanctuary. Arietta, the owner of Beachy Bakes, had become a business-owning mentor of sorts. But it was also the boardwalk where Sunlit and Fish had first run into the tall, irritable lady.

With Joy watching over the porpoises—and guarding the pier—Chip and Fish took over the dinner mission. While Biscuit soared overhead, they led the way down the boardwalk, comparing notes about things babies of all species might eat. Together they were the most natural sight in the world; in fact, Chip was officially Fish's adoptive father, though Sunlit had also played an important role in looking after Fish in his early days. They'd both remained so involved with the Sanctuary and Sunlit that she could only be happy about the way things had turned out. Seeing them laughing warmed her heart.

Her mind, however, was still inclined to worry. Sunlit hung back a little with Ige, the irritable stranger forefront in her thoughts.

"You recognized her, right? You said so. I didn't, really, until after she was already mad," she said to him, keeping her voice low.

"Clementina," Ige confirmed. "If you ask me, *mad* is the most recognizable thing about her. Taiwo says it's just because she hates the beach, though. They say she's lovely whenever the council's discussing anything else."

"Why live here?" Sunlit asked, momentarily bewildered.

Ige shrugged as they moved through the crowd. During the summer, nights in Seaside were long and colorful. "Not sure. Something about her family having deep roots here, maybe? Unless someone's bothering with the lifeguards, I usually ignore all that political stuff."

With that philosophy, Sunlit was glad to agree. "Do you think she will, though—bother with the Sanctuary, I mean. Because we were negligent or something?"

"She might." Ige gave Sunlit a look she was familiar with: one dark eyebrow raised, bald head at an angle, lips parted as though something was on the tip of his tongue but he was choosing his next words carefully nonetheless. "You think either Officer Ebb or Taiwo will actually believe her?"

Fretting already, Sunlit did not notice that this was a question meant to have an obvious answer. "When Fish first came last year, we ran into her and got water all over her dress, and now it's happened again," she said. "Taiwo said she was behind some of the—you know, the—the way some people were unpleasant, and all the rumors about curses."

"Yeah," Ige said dryly, "from what I gather, Clementina's not one to suffer in silence. But don't you think that means that Ebb and everyone on town council are used to her by now?"

This time, Sunlit caught on to the fact that she was being quizzed. But she still hesitated, nearly running into a set of grandparents and grandchildren who were throwing darts at balloons full of paint. "I don't know, I just—I just don't want to cause trouble," she said, a little lamely, unwilling to give a wrong answer.

"Maybe close the pier gate while the porpoises are here," Ige suggested. "Trust me, word's going to get out about them. You might find you have way more visitors than you want."

"Why?" Sunlit frowned.

Ige gestured at a nearby stall which sold towels that, when thrown over the head, made the wearer look like a whale or dolphin or porpoise. Then he pointed at a passing child clutching a porpoise stuffie, and another shop whose sign read *Seaside Charms for Every Porpoise.*

". . . Oh," said Sunlit. "You think they'll be popular? But they really shouldn't be subjected to noise and excitement right now." Memories of Zila's reaction to Clementina only underscored that fact.

"So, close your gate," Ige repeated patiently. "I'll help enforce it, but you have to do it first."

"We did tonight, anyway," Sunlit said, half to herself. "Okay, we'll keep it that way. But what should I tell people who ask?"

Ige smirked. "Tell them you have a kraken back there."

Sunlit considered pointing out that this made no sense. There was barely room in the annex for a *baby* kraken, at best. But thoughts of baby krakens naturally led to thoughts of Fish, and there he was just ahead of them, waving excitedly in front of a sushi stand.

And the stall right next door, Sunlit couldn't help but notice, advertised extra-creamy coconut milkshakes in ninety-nine flavors, plus disintegrating straws.

* * *

Full of mango-avocado rolls and sipping a peanut butter milkshake, Sunlit sat on the lifeguard station looking over the darkened beach with her friends. Biscuit whirled, a blue shape against the moon, and perched on the railing behind them.

"*Sherbet!*" the parrot squawked. "*Fish!*"

"*Biscuit!*" Fish parroted back, his short legs kicking against the platform they sat on.

"Sherbet" was the name Sunlit's grandmother had called her, one Biscuit had learned long ago. It made her wonder what her grandmother would think if she could see Marine Sanctuary now.

"*Porpoises!*" Biscuit added.

Chip took a long sip of his acid wildberry smoothie—guaranteed not to have any *real* acid in it, of course. "You should put Biscuit in charge of your marketing, Sunlit."

"Maybe she doesn't want marketing," Ige suggested.

"Maybe we'd know that if you didn't talk for her," Chip retorted.

The two of them, sitting beside each other in the middle of the little line, smiled at each other.

Sunlit, on Ige's other side, now contemplated the sliver of moon above them. Her left hand ached terribly—though the coolness of the milkshake in its charmed paper cup was helpful. She couldn't help but think about the full sun the porpoises would be exposed to, in the annex the next morning. That seemed like a more important question than marketing. The baby's skin was already dehydrated enough.

But in the past year of living in Seaside, she'd learned that if she asked the right question, sometimes the answer presented itself. She'd also learned that if Chip and Ige were not interrupted, they'd bicker (lovingly) all night.

"Are there any shops on the boardwalk that sell shade spells?" she asked.

If the question seemed sudden, nobody showed it. Chip leaned out thoughtfully so that he could see her. "There's parasols, aren't there? The school kids did an art project where they each got to decorate one."

"I made mine the deep ocean!" added Fish, from his point on the far end. His vanilla cake crumble milkshake was nearly gone, and his straw rattled as he strained to pick up the last drops.

"That sounds cool," Sunlit said, and meant it. "But I was thinking of something bigger."

"For the annex?" Ige was used to anticipating problems.

"If that's what you want, wasn't there an old sail in that pile of junk leftover from the damage on the pier?" Chip asked.

Sunlit thought about it. After the pier's cleanup last spring, she had kept some "potentially useful" items in the shop just in case. Last she remembered, Joy had used the sail as a cape at a Halloween party. "I think it's still around. You think it could be strung up? But the annex has no mast any more."

"It has just enough," Chip said cheerfully. "All you'd have to do is hook a rod through the bottom end of the sail, so it keeps its shape. Since the mast is at the back of the boat, you secure the rod to the mast, crosswise, and tie down the top of the sail to something tall at the front, and there you go!"

"It wouldn't be very far off the water," Sunlit mused, "but I guess it wouldn't have to be . . ."

"Something to think about tomorrow," Ige suggested, swirling his salted caramel milkshake. He still had half of his left.

"Add it to the list," Chip agreed. "You sure you can manage all the work now that the porpoises are here, Professor?"

"There's Joy too," Sunlit said automatically. "Most of the work is just making sure the baby gets regular food at this point. And trying out different skin treatments. And making sure any other complications are dealt with."

"And keeping people off the pier," Ige reminded her.

"Still." Sunlit hesitated. "Thank you—all of you for helping settle them in."

"You got the milkshakes," Chip reminded her with a grin. "That's thanks enough for me."

"*Many hands!*" Biscuit screeched.

"Exactly," said Ige, with a pointed look at Sunlit. "Don't worry about asking for help. Maybe next time," he added, glancing at Chip, "you might even get a proper permit for boating by the beach."

7

A Lovelorn Letter

> *With some treatments, there is a fine line between the medical and the purely cosmetic. If you have an animal patient who can not speak for itself, be careful that you are not making preemptive decisions. Sometimes what seems cosmetic could be necessary for an animal's survival. Sometimes, however, a needless procedure may do more harm than good.*
>
> *—from* Standard Practices for a Safe & Sanitary Animal Medic

Sunlit appreciated Ige's point. She'd learned a lot during her time in Seaside, things she never could have appreciated in a university class.

But she also hadn't *quite* gotten over her determination to see things done.

After Ige, Chip, and Fish dropped her and Biscuit off at the

Sanctuary, Sunlit checked on Joy, who volunteered to take the night shift feeding the baby. The otter naturally slept in short stretches and often liked to look after creatures who needed care during the night, as it gave her something to do while she was up stretching her legs. This was a great help to Sunlit, of course, but it did mean that any food that involved more preparation than serving up bits of fish had to be made ahead of time.

Over the past year, Marine Sanctuary had become an extension of Sunlit's self. Even in the dark, it was easy to navigate. The front wall, facing a wide open deck at the bottom of the boardwalk, boasted a barn-style door and rows of charmed, stacked fish tanks. Along the back wall was a large L-shaped counter and sinks for both fresh and saltwater, and a back door which opened directly above the annex. Beside that was a partitioned-off area which Sunlit used as her exam room, and on the far side was another barn door opening beside the gate to the Sanctuary's private pier. For a simple rectangle built as a bait shop, the building served surprisingly well. And via a hatch in the ceiling above the counter was the attic, now transformed into Sunlit's studio apartment.

Though Biscuit immediately disappeared up into the rafters of the attic, Sunlit stayed at the counter to mix up porpoise food for Joy to use. The otter herself had gone out for a quick swim after promising to take night shift, so the Sanctuary was quiet. This was perhaps Sunlit's favorite time of day in her little rescue shelter.

Though she'd spent years studying, Sunlit sometimes felt intimidated by the titles others gave her—like Chip calling her "professor," or children off the beach bringing her a tired jellyfish because she was a "vet." Technically Seaside did have a true veterinarian, a rather crusty, rather large werebear who was by all accounts quite competent, but refused to deal with marine animals. Sunlit personally thought of herself just as a marine biologist, a researcher. But in the forgiving silence of her Sanctuary, she could do her best to be whatever her animals needed.

By the time she'd mixed up the last bottle and stored it in the icebox under the counter, Joy had returned and was ready for a pre-night watch nap beside the pier gate. And since she was on her own (parrot notwithstanding), Sunlit decided to do something she knew everyone else would give her a hard time for.

She stayed up just a little later and put the sail up herself.

The first task was simply to locate the sail. Storage space was limited to a few shelves in the exam room and whatever they could stuff under the counter, a task made more difficult by the sheer vastness of the old ice box which had once been used to store bait. But the counter itself was deep, and after rummaging for a long time past boxes of sunscreen and safety brochures, Sunlit finally found the crumpled piece of heavy canvas shoved into a back corner. When it fell over her boots as it came loose from its haphazard folding, she realized that Chip had been right: it would easily cover a large section of the annex—or at least the shallow end of it. That was the most important part. The tricky thing now was to make sure the sail kept its triangular shape, just as Chip had suggested.

Sunlit cast her eyes around the darkened Sanctuary, wondering what she could use as a rod. Eventually, her eyes lighted on a long pole in the corner by the exam room. It had been leftover when they'd made the gate, and she'd kept it in case the gate needed reinforcement. So far the gate was working fine, and

Sunlit felt confident about repurposing the pole now. Using twine they kept on hand, Sunlit tied first one corner of the sail and then the other to the pole, and carefully carried the whole thing out the back door to set it all up.

Of course, setting it up was *not* as simple nor nearly as easy a task as Chip had made it sound. Especially with a tender, burned hand. But Sunlit was determined, and after quite a bit of heaving and wriggling and splashing about, she managed to get the sail into place so that it covered all of the baby porpoise's shelf and a good deal of the boat's middle, too. In the weak moonlight, the effect was murky shadow, but Sunlit was reasonably certain that the sail would hold. Fortunately, there was no rain or high wind in the forecast.

And with that comforting thought, she finally climbed up to her bed in the attic, finally dressed her burned hand, and promptly fell asleep.

The next morning, Sunlit descended to work cautiously, but Joy made no comment on the sail. Her nose twitched as she saw Sunlit, and Sunlit fought the urge to hide her medicated glove behind her back. But again, the otter said nothing except,

"Good morning! You're up early. It's just about time to feed the baby again. If you want to do that, I'll head out for a swim."

"By all means," Sunlit said, relieved. "When you get back I have an errand to run, is all. I figured yesterday I should write to Professor Lina and see about some emergency supplies."

"Always good to be prepared," Joy commented, nuzzling Sunlit's shoulder affectionately before she slipped out the door.

With that, Sunlit wholeheartedly agreed. She mixed up the baby porpoise's food for the day, gathered a selection of aquatic skincare balms, and made her way down to the annex.

She'd managed to coat both porpoises in one skin cream

yesterday, before leaving for dinner. But because she'd never had to deal with magical technicolor animals, she wasn't sure which cream would actually work. Her first choice had been a multi-purpose rehydration cream, which turned out to have had very healing effects on the baby porpoise's dry patches, but no effect whatsoever on its color. Today Sunlit decided to go a step further. Sitting in the shallows next to the baby's tub, she pulled the lid off of a huge tub of medical color correction cream.

It was meant to be used on scar tissues, to ease the exposed skin and lessen the startling effects of, say, a bright white line on an otherwise black or grey animal. This wasn't just a cosmetic practice: animals who relied on the pigments in their skin to conceal themselves from predators or prey, for example, could find their lives impacted by an old, poorly healed injury.

Sunlit used her injured hand to hold the tub steady, applying cream to the baby—and then to an impatient Zila—using only her right hand. It made an already awkward process even slower, but the added time was worth the risk of exposing her already-burned skin.

She'd just finished up as Joy returned, leaping smoothly up onto the end of the pier. The otter trotted over to the annex, pausing to cock her head down at Sunlit.

"You've already got a crowd," she observed.

"Have we?" Sunlit was surprised: she hadn't even glanced toward the beach yet.

"News travels fast," Joy said, stretching. "Maybe they'll buy some sunscreen."

Sunlit scrambled up onto the pier and peered down toward the boardwalk gate, where Joy was looking. Half a dozen people of various shapes and sizes lingered there, craning their necks.

They waved when they saw Sunlit. One had a rainbow umbrella hat on. Another was wearing a porpoise pin the size of Biscuit's head.

Sunlit gulped and withdrew behind Joy's furry shoulder. "Who *are* they? What do they want?"

"To see a tie dye porpoise," Joy answered, as though it was perfectly relatable.

"But they can't. After yesterday—the last thing we need—"

"Calm down, kit," Joy said soothingly, curling her tail around so that it nudged Sunlit back into the present. "They're behind the gate. And do any of them look like they're about to take on a giant otter?"

Sunlit sighed. Though she knew Joy had a point, she couldn't help but glance at Zila, who was hiding in the shade beside the baby's tub. "I'm sorry, Joy. You're right. I just have a bad feeling about all of this."

"You're just extra protective," Joy replied, with the air of a know-it-all. When Sunlit shook her head in confusion, the otter added, "The baby? You were the same when we had Fish here. There's nothing wrong with it, kit."

"I *do* feel awful for them both," Sunlit admitted. "And it really doesn't help that I don't know how to *help* them. Not really."

"You're doing everything you need to. And more," Joy said, casting one dark eye meaningfully at the sail. "Go on your errand, clear your head. I can handle things here."

"I'll get back soon so you can rest," Sunlit promised.

"Take your time," Joy insisted. Her nose twitched as she looked back toward the little group of onlookers. "Do you smell cinnamon? Maybe one of them will try to bribe me with food."

"Joy!"

"Teasing," the otter said lightly. "But maybe we can turn their interest in porpoises into an interest for the Sanctuary. Something to think about!"

As Sunlit stowed her things and hurried out of the Sanctuary—carefully taking the door farthest from the porpoise enthusiasts—she mulled over this last idea. She stole a glance at the crowd as she snuck down the boardwalk. She didn't recognize anyone there, except for in the vaguest sense of having seen them on the beach before. That meant they hadn't been to the Sanctuary before.

Maybe there was something in what Joy had said, but Sunlit wasn't sure how to accomplish the feat. How would she make strangers care about the Sanctuary?

Much easier to focus on people she *knew* would care.

Walking through town with her hat tipped down, Sunlit mentally rehearsed the letter she'd send to her old professor. She'd been through Seaside so often at this point that she had no need to look around. Behind the boardwalk, the town was arranged along a haphazard main street that paralleled the beach, with side streets and alleys leading to neighborhoods further inland. The buildings all had steep roofs to ward off the heavy rains, and many sported anchors, oars, or even entire ships as decoration—not to mention colorful coats of paint and eclectic window displays. The sandy street was full of tourists—tourists on bikes, tourists on foot, tourists on magical wheelchairs of spinning orbs of water. Most townsfolk tried to do their running-about early in the morning, to beat what they affectionately called "rush hours."

Sunlit wasn't too concerned with the latest craze in swimsuits or the new treats offered at the cafe. She beat the familiar path to the post office, a one-story thatched-roof building on the northern end of town. Keeping her hands well hidden from the sun and her thoughts on her task, she moved with purpose. Should she start with some kind of pleasantries? Usually she just got to the point. But it had been a while since she'd last written. It had been—oh dear—maybe as long ago as the penguin incident? That had been over the winter . . .

Deep in her thoughts, Sunlit didn't notice Rachel until she stepped on the bookseller's strappy purple sandals.

"I'm sorry," Sunlit said automatically, blushing even more furiously when she realized who she'd run into.

"In a hurry?" Rachel returned, smiling faintly. She'd just emerged from the post office. A bundle of packages and newspapers was tucked under her arm. Though her black scholarly robes looked as hot as ever, she looked perfectly cool behind her blue ombre glasses. Tiny seashells decorated the edges of the frame.

"I—I have a letter to write," Sunlit said, trying to hide the fact that she suddenly felt like a collection of loose ends rather than a competent biologist.

"You know, you could keep stationery in the Sanctuary," Rachel told her. "I have lots on sale at the store."

"I always forget." Indeed, Sunlit was accustomed to writing her letters using the post office's standard envelopes and paper, sitting at the tables outside the little building. Paper was one of those things she just couldn't seem to keep on hand. But she couldn't say that to *Rachel* of all people.

Rachel apparently wasn't done talking, though. She touched Sunlit's arm, guiding her to one side of the post office's wide open doors, so that they were out of the way of traffic. "How are the porpoises doing?"

Sunlit had to remind herself that "porpoises" were marine

mammals and that she currently was in charge of two, on account of her running a marine sanctuary, and she was frustrated with herself for her own lack of acuity. "Um, ah, they're fine. Not fine really, but they're resting, which is good. Everyone's good. Joy and I have been taking turns feeding the baby."

"The baby *porpoise*, right?" Rachel's brow momentarily creased.

Though her statement *had* been ambiguous, Sunlit frowned. Had Rachel not even noticed that one of the porpoises was a baby? "Of course. Why else would we have one?"

"I don't know," Rachel said, leaning back a little. "Are you sure you're doing okay? You seem like maybe you're having a bad day."

"I'm fine," Sunlit said, abashed. "How are you?"

"I'm good. I'm seeing Mouse again later," Rachel said, momentarily lightening. Then, glancing around, she added, "So the rumors aren't true, then?"

"What rumors? About the porpoises?" Sunlit swayed a little.

"No, about the Sanctuary. This morning at the cafe I heard . . ." Rachel looked at her with trepidation. "Well, I don't want to make things worse."

Sunlit was convinced things were already terrible. "What rumors?"

"Just that . . . someone had been injured on the pier, and was going to sue for it. Or something like that," Rachel ended hurriedly. "If you haven't heard anything about it, though, I wouldn't worry."

Of course Sunlit's mind jumped instantly to Clementina. But there wasn't anything she wanted to say on the subject.

"In any case, I hope your day gets better," Rachel said. "I

should get to the bookstore—it's almost opening time. Tell Joy I said hi, okay?"

Sunlit murmured something appropriate, then stood contemplating the door to the post office as Rachel set off.

Crowds, rumors, porpoises, Mouse . . .

She shook her head. The important thing right now was emergency supplies, and that meant writing a letter. Everything else would have to wait.

8

A New Conversation

> *For the tourist intent on getting a feel for local life—and local food—a visit to Seaside's marina is a must. The fish market was recently renovated and boasts every kind of seafood imaginable, including many magical ingredients. Indeed, rumor has it that there was a period of time when a covert market sold questionable items to unscrupulous folks . . . but those days are long gone!*
>
> *—from* A Guide to Seaside (for the Discerning Tourist)

Sunlit returned to Marine Sanctuary just in time for the baby porpoise's next feeding. The crowd of onlookers had multiplied and some had moved inside. Joy was cheerful behind the counter, selling sunscreen and handing out brochures. She nodded briefly when Sunlit slipped into the exam room to get a fresh bottle. Though Sunlit hesitated, wondering if Joy needed a break, the otter resolutely ignored her, and Sunlit got the hint: the porpoises came first. In that, she and Joy were on the same page.

Rather than clambering past the otter to get to the back door, Sunlit took the wiser course of heading out the side door and down the pier. Per her new habit, she made sure the gate was closed and locked behind her.

Zila was resting in the mid-morning sun, the skin salve glowing faintly blue over his green-splotched back. He lifted his head as she approached and followed her progress toward the back of the boat, where the baby still lay in its tub.

Sunlit's boots sloshed through the water as she let herself down onto the submerged deck. The sudden cool sensation was one she'd grown to love. Going from dry and hot to cool and wet invariably meant shifting her focus from other people to marine creatures, which was a relief. Though Sunlit loved her friends in Seaside dearly—some too dearly, apparently—she did often feel overwhelmed or uncertain what to do with them. With animals, she could usually figure it out.

Usually.

But Joy had been right to point out that things weren't so bad, even if Sunlit wasn't sure exactly what was going on with her charges. The baby porpoise, for example, was already showing signs of improvement. The sail erected as a shade had been a difficult feat, but an excellent idea. Shielded from the sun and covered in cream, the rough dryness was nearly all gone from the baby's back, and its little tub was a reasonable temperature, only slightly warmer than the rest of the annex. Best of all, when the tiny porpoise caught wind of the bottle, it lifted its head all on its own to begin feeding.

Sunlit watched the baby carefully, aware that Zila was watching her. Like the adult porpoise, the baby's skin was still covered in glowing water-proof cream. But the treatment was not fully opaque, which made examining its skin still possible. Sunlit could see very clearly that the color-changing effects had not receded yet; yellow, then orange, then purple chased each other over the porpoise's back.

Already in a pensive mood, Sunlit had to admit the obvious to herself. It was possible the effect would never recede. But . . . did that need to be a bad thing?

"I don't know, Zila," Sunlit murmured as the baby ate. "You two might just always be the most colorful porpoises out there. As long as other porpoises still recognize you, and it doesn't make you more prone to predator attacks . . ."

Zila whistled. Sunlit wasn't sure what he meant or which one of them he was whistling at, but she turned her head and smiled at him. "You're safe right in this moment, at least. That's what matters, right? And you have each other. Speaking of . . ." To distract herself from the slightly prickly idea of *each other*, Sunlit looked down at the baby again. "I can't go on saying 'the baby porpoise' forever. It's so *long*. But apparently, just saying 'the baby' is problematic too. I wish you'd tell me your baby's name, Zila."

The complaint was mostly rhetorical. Though Sunlit could often interpret animals' own names, she'd never gotten other names or words from them—just feelings. Unless, of course, the animal could talk.

She had to smile at that. In her days at the university, she'd often preferred to work with non-magical animals; their care was more straightforward. Or at least, that was how she'd felt at the time. Now, she had to admit that it could be very nice and simple, dealing with someone like Joy who could tell her exactly what was wrong (and all her thoughts on the matter, besides!).

"Can I give your baby a nickname, Zila?" Sunlit asked on a whim, looking up.

Though again she expected no direct answer, the porpoise seemed to survey her carefully out of one beady eye.

"It's just a term of—of affection, really," Sunlit explained to him. "It could be something very silly. Chip—you met Chip yesterday—he calls me the 'Professor,' even though I'm not really. So it doesn't have to be *true*.

"Come to think of it, he didn't even ask me first, either," Sunlit mused.

"Chip!" On vibrant blue wings, Biscuit flew down from the Sanctuary's attic, joining the scene. He perched on the derelict mast above the sail, a shadowy shape against the cloth. *"Fish and chips!"*

"Are you thinking of friends, or just food?" Sunlit asked, teasing him. She'd also never been sure how purposeful Biscuit's "parroting" was, but it was fun to have him around.

Fun.

"Granola," Biscuit replied.

Sunlit laughed. "Nobody here likes that but you. But I guess that answers the question." And now *she* was thinking of friends. Chip, Fish, and Ige were all constant sources of wonder in her life. Maybe Chip hadn't been wrong. Maybe even if one thing didn't work out, other things made up for it.

The baby porpoise tugged at the bottle, which was empty now. Sunlit chuckled softly as she pulled it back. "No more right now, friend," she said. "We wouldn't want you to add too much weight gain to your other problems—especially when you're not getting a lot of exercise. Would you like to come out for a moment?"

She offered her uninjured hand to the little porpoise, and for a moment, it did show interest—nudging her fingers with its small snout. Gently, she tickled along its chin and played with its flipper, to see if it would keep responding. The baby leaned into her hand.

Tired. The feeling hit Sunlit hard, but she was glad to get it.

"You and me both," she told it gently. "There's a lot going on. But you'll be okay here. You can rest. Your parent is right here. Want to see him?"

With steady movements, she shifted her hands to hold the little porpoise and lifted it from the tub, ignoring the sting of saltwater. She set the baby on her knees, so that it was submerged but could still breathe easily.

Zila had been waiting there all along, of course, and now nuzzled the baby curiously from the deeper water beyond Sunlit's feet. Listening to the chirruping and clicks gave Sunlit a feeling of eavesdropping on a family conversation, but she had to see if the baby made noise back. Anything was progress. The little porpoise didn't speak, but it did snuggle with its father from the safety of Sunlit's lap.

Its breathing became slower, and—Sunlit stroked her fingertips along its back, wondering. Had the color changes slowed, too? They still moved across its skin, arched around its little belly.

"Rainbow," she decided. "That's what I'll call you, until you tell me otherwise."

Zila, pressed up against her knees, was more relaxed now too. Sunlit watched the two of them for a moment before smiling. In a minute, she'd go into the store and take over for Joy so that the otter could finally rest. But for now, it was quiet. She settled herself into a more comfortable sitting position on the deck and let the porpoises sleep.

* * *

Sunlit was just finishing a cheese and cress sandwich that afternoon when Officer Ebb arrived at the Sanctuary.

He didn't barge in—his manner was as muted and respectable as always. But he did cast a sideways glance at the tourists gazing into the tanks, something that made Sunlit's heart rate pick up. What might he have to say that he didn't want others to overhear? Whatever it was, he waited until he was leaning over the counter toward her to speak.

"I need your help in the marina," he said, keeping his voice low. "Any chance you can get away for a minute?"

"Joy is outside," Sunlit said. "I'll just close up in here. If you think it'll be quick? Is there an animal involved?"

"Yes to both," said Officer Ebb. "I hope."

With this vague reassurance, Sunlit set about preparation. Fortunately, the group of tourists was just leaving, having had their fill of the salamander, saturn snail, and Biscuit. Sunlit followed them to the side door and pulled the bottom half of it closed, leaning out to tell Joy she'd be back shortly. When she rejoined Ebb at the counter, she paused. "Will I need to bring anything?"

"If you have something for first aid?" Officer Ebb suggested. "I don't know for sure if there's any injury yet to worry about."

Sunlit made herself pause a moment longer. She'd learned from her experience with the porpoises. "What kind of animal is it? What's happened?"

"A sizable gray seal," Officer Ebb answered, tugging at one

ear as though out of his depth. "There's been a bit of an accident in the marina, but reports say it's just trapped."

This was useful information, though her heart went out to the seal. Sunlit scooped some items from her exam room into her bag, crammed a wide-brimmed hat onto her head, and followed Officer Ebb out, careful to lock the front door on her way.

He set out from Marine Sanctuary and took a right, away from the boardwalk. As they climbed the wide steps that led to the town's recently-built fishing marina, protected by a high breakwater, Officer Ebb explained a little more. "One of the sailors ran up to the police station just now and told me about everything I've told you. I figured I'd better get you on the way down. Save some time."

"It does make sense," Sunlit agreed. As they climbed, the masts of boats returned from their early morning fishing trips came into view. "Although if we have to move the seal, we'll still need more help. Probably I'd have to trade places with Joy . . ."

"True," said Officer Ebb, giving her one of his thoughtful looks. "But let's hope it doesn't come to that."

By then, they'd reached the top of the stairs. From their vantage point they could look out along the breakwater, which sheltered the boats and, to some extent, Marine Sanctuary and its annex, nestled along the outside of the rocky wall. In front of them, though, was a wide new pier wholly unlike the boardwalk. Metal-railed staircases led down to floating docks in orderly rows, and boats were lined up among them like chess pieces on a board. A long, low-slung building stood between the marina and the street, its sides open to the air, letting out a thick smell of fresh fish. This was the market where the sailors brought their catch.

Sunlit rarely had to come up here, because Chip often made seafood deliveries himself—especially since she wasn't picky about what the Sanctuary got, unless they had a very specific animal to feed. She looked at Officer Ebb. Fortunately, he was familiar with all aspects of Seaside life. He set off with ease, as though he walked these docks every day.

Ebb strode to the farthest staircase, along the southern end of the marina, and started down it at a trot, taking the corrugated steps two at a time. Sunlit was not nearly so graceful, but she did her best to keep up. By now, she had an inkling where they were headed. At the end of the dock there was a boat at an odd angle and much shouting going on.

She and Officer Ebb walked out along the dock to join a small circle of very agitated folk.

One was standing at the prow of a tethered boat, hands on ample hips, in coarse green overalls and with a poof of curly black hair tied back into a ponytail. *Maryanna,* said a name tag sewn into her overalls, and she was yelling ferociously at an older merperson in sailor's clothes while a small, slight sailor covered in colorful tattoos looked on.

"Alright, alright," said Officer Ebb, and his voice cut through the mayhem at once. "What's happened here?"

The mayhem began again.

"This *pleasure cruise* came waltzing in here—"

"—it should be against marina rules to just lay things out everywhere—"

"—just trying to dry my nets in peace—"

"Wait," Sunlit cried, interrupting Maryanna and the merfolk captain. Before she could second-guess her own audacity, she went on, "is there an animal hurt here?"

All three guilty parties turned as one. Between Maryanna's boat, which was docked and holding fast, and the merfolk captain's long, shallow boat, which was lodged between the end of the dock and the stone breakwater with its oars at odd angles, a very large spotted seal was bobbing in the water. When it saw them all looking at it, it barked back.

"From here, I don't see anything wrong with it," Sunlit said, brow creased. "Why hasn't it swum away, under the boats?"

"A very good question," Officer Ebb added, fixing both captains with a stare. "Ombo, you first."

The merfolk captain, whose nearly ink-black skin and sapphire scales looked roughened by saltwater and time, smoothed his long tunic over his belly. "Officer Ebb, we're here on *business*, Sandy and me. We had an appointment to come in here and pick somebody up. But we got off-course and overshot the pier—it could happen to anybody!"

"And you?" Officer Ebb turned to Maryanna.

"*I* was minding my own business, cleaning up for the day," she said hotly. One eye flashed gold, the other deep brown. "I had the pier to myself and all the nets laid out. Then *these* reckless lubbers crash into the pier and scrape my nets off with them!"

"And a seal that size just happened to be nearby, right in the way?" Sunlit was fairly certain no one was sharing the whole story.

Ombo looked at his fellow sailor, Sandy, who looked down at the dock under their feet. "I was following it."

"Following a seal, instead of watching the docks!" Ombo sounded disgusted.

Briefly, Sandy protested. "I wanted to see how close we could get!"

"So you chased the seal over here and the nets got tangled up on your oars and boat, trapping it," Officer Ebb surmised. He glanced at Sunlit. "Any ideas?"

"Well, this kind of seal is not going to be able to escape by coming up onto the dock," Sunlit said, reasoning it out even as she made a note in the back of her mind: *ask Rachel about making a brochure on animals and boating safety.* "The distance is too high for it to jump, especially if it can't go down very far beneath the surface to get up speed. So we really need to get the nets out of the way, assuming the seal is otherwise fine. I can try to take a closer look at it, but in the meantime . . ."

"One of you is going to have to free those nets, anyway," Officer Ebb concluded, looking back at the sailors.

"You know I can't swim any more," Ombo said to Sandy, still a little harsh. But for a merperson who couldn't swim, for whatever reason, Sunlit suddenly understood why he might be frustrated at this situation. "Go on. It's your mess."

"And don't you dare do any more damage to my nets!" Maryanna added for good measure.

Sandy, accepting their fate, sighed and jumped into the water, holding on to the boat as they began to tug at the tangled nets.

At Officer Ebb's nod, both Maryanna and Ombo went to the dock to keep watch over this procedure. To Sunlit, the officer explained, "Swimming's usually too dangerous around here with all the traffic—strictly against the rules. But sometimes, needs must. We just try to be careful. We can leave the nets to them, if you want to look at the seal?"

Sunlit was already moving to the dock's edge, between the two boats. She let her feet into the water slowly so as not to scare the animal, and pulled some fish from her bag. This seal was wild enough that she didn't try to hand-feed it; instead, through strategic fish-tossing, she was able to examine most of its body from a slight distance. She let the others' conversation fade as she focused.

Officer Ebb crouched beside her after a while. "They've nearly got the nets free," he said. "

"Good. Letting him swim out himself would be much better than trying to pull him out of here," Sunlit replied. "He seems perfectly fine, just agitated, which is understandable. Does . . . this sort of thing happen often?"

"Trust me, you'd know if it did," Ebb returned with a slight grin.

Sunlit glanced away from the seal to catch his expression. "I suppose that's true, but it just seems so . . . *weird.*"

"Nautical accidents defy weird," said Ebb, with a hint of long experience behind the words. "Honestly, I was expecting *more* disturbances like this when they built the new pier. But Del Sol Development put a lot of effort into the planning, with the town's help, of course. On the whole, it's a well-designed place and it's run just fine."

"Until a seal gets in," Sunlit couldn't help but comment.

"Precisely." Officer Ebb gave her that thoughtful look again. "You know, Ombo's on the town council."

"With Taiwo?" *And Clementina?* Sunlit didn't ask.

"Yes, and others," said Ebb, amused. "He mentioned something to me just now about another project from Del Sol. Have they approached you about it?"

"Me?" Sunlit was startled. "No. Should they? Why, for consultation about the animals?"

"Something like that," said Ebb. "Nothing's been proposed yet. I wouldn't worry."

9

A Rude Awakening

The spotted seal is one of the more charismatic species. Though generally found alone, they have been known to take a liking to members of other species—humans, whales, or even boats, for example. One became so bonded with a sorcerer that he eventually learned to talk. Most suspect a spell of some kind was involved . . .

—*from* Traverse's Guide to Marine Vertebrates, Invertebrates, and Magical Outliers

When the nets were freed and the seal was let loose, rocketing through the water and out of the marina, Sunlit did forget to worry. She returned to the Sanctuary for a quiet night, and the next morning found her deep asleep in her attic apartment.

Like the porpoises not so far away, she was cozy and warm. As a matter of fact, Sunlit's attic had benefited from her friends' expertise and generosity—and her own resourcefulness—as much as her annex had. What had once been bare boards and dust bunnies now boasted a snug sleeping corner with an old ship's bed, a fully functional bathroom and a tiny kitchen, and even a few thrifted sofas and a shelf of books placed strategically near a window. On long, quiet evenings, Sunlit could sometimes be found lounging there.

This morning, however, she was not lounging as much as hiding under her blankets from the light pouring through the windows. As soon as Joy woke her with the morning's news, she'd wish she could have stayed there!

Joy's knock at the hatch that led down into the Sanctuary was a familiar one. Even had it not been effective, it immediately set off Biscuit, who slept in the attic's rafters.

"*Morning!*" the parrot squawked. "*Good morning!*"

"Not exactly," Joy said, poking her head up under the door just enough that her dark eyes and whiskers were visible. Sunlit peeked out from her cover to meet the otter's gaze.

"What's the matter?" she asked sleepily. "Is it time for me to take over the feeding schedule?"

"Yes, and," said Joy.

Sunlit sat up, rubbing at her eyes. "And what?"

"Something new has happened," said Joy.

This snapped Sunlit to attention. "Is it a new animal?"

"*Animal! Furry animal!*" Biscuit added.

"He really is lucky I can't fit up there," Joy said conversationally. "No, it's not a new animal. You'll just have to come down, I'm afraid. I thought of taking them down myself, but it's better you should know."

Sunlit did not care for enigmas in the morning—or really any time. She cleaned up and got dressed quickly, swinging herself down behind the counter. Hungry fish and a cheerful salamander watched her from the tanks along the wall; she'd feed them in a minute. Hopefully. Unless whatever Joy had found would take too long—?

Joy herself was outside the side door. Full of nerves, Sunlit tugged her sun hat and gloves into place. Was it a crowd already? Even though Sunlit had slept in a bit, it was still long before most people were on the beach.

When she got outside, what she found was not at all what she expected.

A dozen signs were posted on the gate, the side of the Sanctuary, and even the railing of the pier, as though an art class had decided to take up residence overnight. But though the posters were colorful, they were *not* joyful. In large block letters of red, black, and yellow, they boasted slogans like,

Marine Sanctuary a HAZARD to visitors!

Old pier blocks progress!

Sick animals should stay off the beach!

Irresponsible care is NO care at all!

No visitors on PORPOISE!

And even:

Sunlit Haven hates FUN!

The slogans seemed to come from all angles—and not just because they'd been haphazardly posted atop one another. Some

Sunlit could see as having potentially come from Clementina and the rumors Rachel had relayed about the pier, but some made no sense to her at all. And some hit far too close to home.

"I don't understand," Sunlit whispered.

"I'm sorry, kit," Joy said, swishing her long tail across the pier as though she might sweep the trouble away. "I slept out in the water by the annex between feedings, and I didn't notice a thing."

Sunlit hugged her arms around herself, her gloves crumpling her heavy linen overalls. "It's not your fault."

What more, she wondered, *was there to say?*

"Oh, dear," said a new—but not strange—voice behind them.

Sunlit wiped her eyes as she turned around. But Arietta had that grandmotherly way that didn't mind a spot of crying one bit. The little gnome reached up to pat Sunlit's arm affectionately as she joined them. "Vandals are never any fun," she said. "But not to worry—Officer Ebb will be after them in a jiffy, if Ige isn't already."

"Do you think they've seen this?" Sunlit's voice wobbled. Just who else *had* seen it?

"If they haven't, they will soon enough," Arietta replied. "The more important thing is whether you've eaten, dear. And you, Joy? How are you these days?"

As she spoke, Arietta acted. On her free arm, she had carried over a basket; from this, she withdrew a fluffy croissant, which she pressed into Sunlit's hands. Arietta ran Beachy Bakes on the boardwalk. She was so wholly on theme with her store that, even out of it, she reminded one of it: her tuft of blue hair rose from her head like frosting, and her light blue eyes precisely matched the paint colors she'd chosen for her business—not to mention the apron which even now she wore over her gingham dress. She was only as tall as Sunlit's thigh, but she'd always had a large presence.

Joy was telling her all about the porpoises. Sunlit discovered she'd eaten half of her croissant, which turned out to have spinach and cheese inside.

"Arietta," she said, hardly aware she was interrupting a conversation, "did you say things like this have happened on the boardwalk before?"

"I wouldn't say *exactly* the same, dearie," Arietta said sympathetically as she turned to eye the signs once more. "But vandalism, it happens every once in a while. There's no accounting for some people, is there?"

"Is that all this is? Vandalism?" Sunlit asked.

"Isn't vandalism when someone paints on something?" Joy added curiously.

"There's that, but it can be more things, too. I can't tell you about all the rules, but I'm sure Ige could," Arietta told them both. "I have to get back to my ovens now, but I'll be sure to come over later, dearie. Why don't you see if you can wave Ige down? I'm sure he'll be on the beach any minute now."

Arietta, as so often happened, was right—it was exactly the time of morning when Ige usually began his shift. (Arietta made a sport of watching the boardwalk and knowing its goings-on.) With this kindly advice and another pastry gift, this one a warm cinnamon roll, Arietta left Sunlit and Joy to contemplate their next move.

"We should feed Rainbow," was all Sunlit could think.

"I'll do that," Joy said. "I was hoping to take a bit of a swim before grooming, anyway."

"Sounds good," Sunlit replied, knowing that Joy meant she would swim out from the annex once she was done with her task. Routines were easy to keep track of. Knowing what to do about *something new*—that was something else entirely.

* * *

"Despicable," was Ige's opinion, when at last Sunlit managed to flag him down. He stood with his hands on his hips, squinting at the signs like they might give up who had made them. "Have you sent for Officer Ebb?"

"No," Sunlit admitted. Mostly, she'd just stood in the shade of the Sanctuary and wondered *why* someone would target it this way. "Joy just finished taking care of the porpoises, and went out. When she gets back I could go over to the station, I guess."

Ige shifted to eye her instead of the signs. "Are the porpoises in so much need of constant care?"

"Not exactly," Sunlit told him. "They're doing pretty well, overall. But yesterday we had a crowd of curious people here, just like you said. So we've been trying to make sure one of us is on hand to deal with that. Although . . . if everybody shows up and sees these signs . . ."

"Don't worry about it," Ige said gruffly. He walked over to the edge of the pier, overlooking the beach, and blew two short trills on his whistle. In no time flat, a trainee lifeguard was barreling toward them.

"Good reaction time, Ismael," Ige said to the panting merfolk recruit. "Run down to the police station, would you? It's not an emergency, but tell Ebb he's needed at Marine Sanctuary."

The recruit saluted and sprinted away.

"Thanks," Sunlit said, still a little in awe of Ige's network of disciplined lifeguards. "Um, what should we do until he gets here?"

"Take the signs down, obviously," Ige said.

"But won't the police need to . . . collect evidence or something?"

"They'll get enough from the posters themselves," Ige said enigmatically. It was all Sunlit needed to hear. She was only too glad to clear such hurtful things off of her pier.

As they worked side by side detaching tape and tacks, Ige added, "By the way, I have a letter for you. It came to the lifeguard station this morning, special post. Why don't you have a post office box set up yet? Or a mailbox for the Sanctuary?"

"It's been on the list." Sunlit waved one hand vaguely. "We don't really need one, normally."

"Think of it more as *I* don't really need your mail showing up at the station," Ige retorted. He caught Sunlit's eye and smirked.

"Fine," she admitted. "I didn't mean to inconvenience you. But right now, we have a lot of other things to deal with."

"I get it, don't worry." Ige piled the last of the posters against the wall, so that their blank backs faced out. Then he handed Sunlit a battered white envelope. "But it wouldn't be terrible to have an official address in Seaside. It's not such a bad place— mostly."

"It isn't," Sunlit agreed, tucking the envelope into a pocket. "And it's not like I'm not committed to the Sanctuary. I just . . ." She hesitated, glancing down at the signs.

"I know. You don't want to cause trouble." Ige sighed. "Sometimes causing trouble is a *good* thing."

Before Sunlit could make sense of this statement—coming from the town lifeguard, no less—Officer Ebb and one of his junior officers arrived.

10

A Sea Away

Imps are small creatures that are made up of elemental magic, like fire or water. They're not skin and bone like you or me! But they love pranks just as much as anybody else, or maybe more.
—from The Children's Encyclopedia of Magical Water Creatures

Officer Ebb was kindly but thorough, as was his wont. He did not, as Sunlit had privately worried, blame the Sanctuary for the vandalism at all; in fact, he offered to post an officer on the pier. Sunlit balked at that, and they settled on having the police swing by often on their rounds. When Officer Ebb took the posters away for analysis, Sunlit felt physical relief.

Still dazed, she waited until after feeding Rainbow to read her letter. She sat partially submerged in the annex, next to Rainbow's tub, as she carefully pulled the letter from the chest pocket on her overalls.

"Here's hoping for good news," she told Zila in a small voice.

The adult porpoise did a sort of cartwheel through the water, splashing both her and the envelope in her hands. Sunlit figured that was about as good a sign as she could hope for, given how her morning was going so far.

As soon as she'd unfolded the letter, her free hand drifted down to Rainbow's tub. Running her fingers gently over the baby's back, sitting comfortably in the shade, she read what her old professor had written:

Haven—

Have had a marvelous idea. Developing a new class for the program, "Practical Rescue and Rehabilitation." Can't think of anyone better suited to guest lecture than yourself. What do you say to a quick visit and one or two lecture slots? Class begins in the fall. Give it some thought.

Sending miracle towels and other things by first parcel post. Keep an eye out for them.

—Lina McAlpin

Sunlit read the letter three times before it sank in.

Then she sat and stared at Zila, who was drifting in meditative circles around the annex.

It will be no surprise, at this point, to mention that Sunlit had a habit of expecting the worst from any given form of communication. It wasn't even really a *habit*, because she was barely aware of this fact about herself, and not at all aware that there was any other way to view communication. In Sunlit's mind, letters were like lightning strikes. She often read them as fast as possible once and then never again, afraid of which sore spot they might expose.

But at the same time, it should be no surprise to say that

Sunlit's ability to predict what someone wanted to say to her was extremely poor. It was hampered, in fact, by her insistence on expecting the worst. As a result, Sunlit was not only habitually worried, but also habitually shocked.

Never, not in a million billion years, would Sunlit have ever thought to think that her old professor might want her to make a *presentation.*

On *rehabilitation.*

Her—the one the signs just this morning called "irresponsible!" The one whose hand was still stuck in a medicated glove!

Sunlit had only wanted some magical conveniences. She had anticipated feeling a bit awkward and guilty for making a request. Mild and familiar sensations, necessary for the good of the Sanctuary. Now she had to restart her heart and make sure she was breathing.

She watched Zila flip, glide, and flip again.

And she was struck by just how far away her old university was.

Literally across a continent, to be precise. On an island which Zila and Rainbow would never swim to, in a whole city of people who knew absolutely nothing about strange acts of vandalism on Seaside's boardwalk. In that moment Sunlit felt very, very small.

Which somehow didn't help her nerves about even being *asked* to speak to undergrads as a "professional" "expert."

She stood abruptly, crumpling the letter and stuffing it back into her pocket. She walked along the boat rail toward the Sanctuary without thinking, with a simple need to *do* something. She'd climbed up the rope ladder and opened the back door to step on a voluminous fluffy tail before she remembered Joy was watching the counter.

"Sorry, sorry," Sunlit murmured, faltering in the transition from bright mid-morning to the Sanctuary's dim interior. She tried stepping over Joy's tail and ended up squishing a paw. "Sorry, I'll get out of your way—"

"I'm in *your* way, kit," Joy said with amusement. She shook herself awake and shifted to let Sunlit in. "Are you coming in for a while? It's been much more quiet today. I could go sun on the pier."

"You could," Sunlit agreed. "That's a good idea. I was just going to—to clean the tanks, and make some more food for Rainbow for later, and go over everything . . ."

Joy's nose twitched as she took in this list. She'd returned from her morning swim in time to hear Ige mention the mail again as he left to take his post on the beach. "Not good news from your professor?"

"What? Um, no, it was fine. She's going to send some things. They might get here tomorrow, we'll have to keep an eye out."

Rising up onto the counter with her front paws for a luxurious stretch, Joy looked down at Sunlit briefly. "Chip'll be by with a seafood delivery soon," she said, "and I suggest you come up with a better cover story by then."

"A better what? A—uh—" Sunlit bit her lip. Joy was already out the back door.

Alone, Sunlit sighed. She tugged off her hat and set it on the counter, running her fingers through her short hair. Joy was right.

There was no keeping secrets from Chip—nor really from Joy, for that matter—nor even from Ige, nor Fish, nor Arietta, who saw everything from her bakery across the way. They'd all find out, one way or another. Just like all those students with all those eyes on her making a presentation. At the thought,

Sunlit wanted to combust.

"*RawwwwwwRR!*"

"Ahhh!" Sunlit jumped and screamed, even though she knew it was only Biscuit. The bird was watching her from one of his favorite perches atop the tanks in the corner. He bobbed his head up and down, suspiciously like laughter.

"Not funny, Biz," Sunlit protested. The parrot had learned that particular trick last spring, from a sick lion seal. He seemed to like it best when the Sanctuary was at its most quiet.

And even though it wasn't funny, he did have a point—sort of. Sunlit reminded herself that she'd come inside to work, not to quietly combust behind the counter. Without another hesitation, she rolled up her sleeves and got down to it.

She'd cleaned out all the inhabited fish tanks and was halfway through refreshing the salamander's sand when someone knocked at the front door frame. Without getting up from her work, Sunlit poked her head up to see Chip leaning in over the half-door.

"Top of the morning to you both," he said, grinning at the salamander atop Sunlit's head.

"I was cleaning, and he can't be in there when I clean," Sunlit explained hastily. She reached up to dislodge the creature, but he was far too comfortable to want to move.

"Sunlit!" Fish burst in through the door, a sphere of water preceding him. Both Sunlit and her salamander reared back: all long-term residents of the Sanctuary were familiar with Fish's unpredictable brand of water magic. "Look, I brought you something! I found it!"

The little boy was obviously proud of himself, but Sunlit couldn't help being confused. "Aren't you supposed to be at school?"

"I *was*," Fish told her, not deterred in the least. "But Teacher said I could leave and do an errand because he was making water shoot up to the ceiling in the middle of lessons!"

"Who was?" Sunlit collected herself, deliberately removing the salamander and putting it safely back in its tank. Then she took a deep breath and peered at Fish's water bubble.

The bubble itself was as big as Fish's head, and he was holding it right in front of his face. The creature inside—because there *was* a creature inside, Sunlit observed as she leaned in—was swimming loops all over the place, like twenty tiny Zilas. But as she traced the movement Sunlit was certain there was only one, and furthermore, she could tell that it was swimming magically rather than physically, with a tail or flippers.

"What is it?" Fish asked her. Then, without waiting for an answer, "Guess where it was!"

Sunlit smiled wryly at Fish, and at Chip behind him. "I think I know. Did you make Chip guess?"

"Only the whole walk here," Chip said affectionately, rubbing Fish's bald head. "Teacher sent a note to the marina, making sure I went over there as soon as I docked."

"I bet." Sunlit reached out and poked the water bubble. In an instant, she had the creature's complete attention. Judging by Fish's impressed reaction, it was the first time the creature had been still all morning. It floated in the water, two legs and two arms and a little head with oversized black eyes. "It's a kind of water imp," Sunlit said with confidence. "I took a whole class on them, a long time ago. I bet you found it in the school's toilet, didn't you?"

"*Cool*," was all Fish said as he stared at the creature.

"Hey, Fish, isn't there a page on imps in your new encyclopedia?" Over the little boy's head, Chip supplied more details.

"From what I heard, it's been causing trouble all morning. Teacher couldn't tell how it had gotten in or what it wanted. No one could catch it but Fish."

"Probably what it wants is a home, or to get back to the home it already has," Sunlit guessed. The water imp, tiring of their scrutiny, attempted to blow a raspberry at her before launching itself at the edges of the bubble again. "They don't talk, generally, but they can be very clever—and very territorial."

Fish was hanging on her every word. "Terry—"

"Territorial," Sunlit repeated, smiling again. "Usually they like freshwater."

"There's all kinds of streams and ponds inland," Chip said thoughtfully. "Not really any on school grounds, though."

"Did it go through the pipes?" Fish asked her.

Sunlit was reminded of a time Fish had helped her get her saltwater pipes up and running, to fill the tanks. "I don't think so, but if we do a little sleuthing we could figure it out. This kind of water imp tends to leave a green scum in the water where it lives. See?"

She pointed at a slimy smudge in the water Fish was holding, which immediately broke the boy's focus. "Yuck!" he declared, as the water bubble popped in his hands. With a splat the imp fell to the floor, where it scrambled upright and began awkwardly squelching away over the wooden floor.

"Catch it again, quick!" Sunlit said, more amused than worried—for once.

Fish leapt after it and contained it again easily. The imp flailed in its new prison.

"Should we be worried about that sludge?" Chip asked, scuffing one sandal at the water marks on the floor.

"It's basically algae," Sunlit replied. "Nothing serious, or too gross. Water imps are purely magical creatures, so they don't eat or defecate." The matter-of-fact way she said this delighted her friends, and amid their merriment, she ushered Fish to an isolated tank under Biscuit's favored corner. "Fish, you can put it in here for now. Chip, will you get us some more fresh water from the tap?"

"Sure thing, Professor," said the sailor, grabbing a nearby bucket from Sunlit's cleaning supplies. "But is it safe? If it could cause mayhem at a school—"

"Schools are sensitive to water imp mayhem," Sunlit replied. "But we know what to do about it here. Right, Fish?"

Fish deposited the imp in the tank and stepped back, his eyes still wide. "What *do* we do?"

Sunlit chuckled. "Nothing, really. The spells on these tanks will contain him just fine. He's only a very little imp and his magic isn't very strong. See?"

Indeed, the imp was racing around his new home only to find, as Sunlit predicted, that nothing he could do would make the glass walls budge.

"We just have to be careful when we pour more water in, and make sure he doesn't escape into the bucket," Sunlit added as Chip came over. Between the three of them, they managed to refresh the imp's new home without mishap.

"Phew." Chip rested the bucket on his hip. "So, what will you do with it?"

"I wasn't kidding about sleuthing," Sunlit said as she stood, too. The imp was safe for now. "I'd like to put it back wherever it came from—which isn't the school, I'm sure, or they'd have noticed it before. I don't think there's anything wrong with it, and it will probably get very bored staying here. Although—"

She crossed to the counter and rummaged in the old drawers.

After a moment she pulled out the string of beads she'd been looking for—a bit of lost-and-found someone had left with them. Perhaps it had been part of a fringed umbrella, or a suncatcher toy. Either way, it would work well as a safe and water-proof distraction now.

"Here, Fish," Sunlit said, holding out the shiny beads. "If you're quick, you can slip these in its tank, too. It might like them."

Fish swelled with importance. He took the string of beads and immediately ran to the imp's tank, pausing just long enough to make sure the imp wouldn't escape before letting the beads fall into the water.

The water imp clamped onto the beads and retreated to a corner.

"All's well so far," Chip said, amused. "Can you leave it there overnight? Fish has to get back to school, and he has a baking date with Arietta this afternoon. How about we go to the bookstore with you tomorrow after school?"

"The bookstore?" Sunlit flushed.

"For a map." Chip gave her a knowing look. "If you want to find where a freshwater critter lives, you'll need more than local oceanic records, right?"

Sunlit looked up at the wall behind the counter, where the tidal maps and seafloor charts Chip referred to had hung ever since the Sanctuary's days as a bait shop. She gulped.

A trip to the bookstore—*that* was an impish project, indeed.

11

A Full Sail

Some of the best things are always the ones you make yourself—memories, drawings, souvenirs. Even better, though, are the ones you make with others.
—from I'm An Adventurer Here Myself

The good thing about the proposed research trip, in Sunlit's view, was that it was scheduled for *tomorrow*. Chip had anticipated that Fish would want to be involved in each step of the process, and he was completely right. Besides, watching the imp overnight just in case any maladies manifested was good practice.

All perfect reasons for putting off a trip to the bookstore.

There was no putting off Chip, though—especially after Joy offered to walk Fish back to school. Sunlit had expected Chip to leave on his own errands as she began to feed the Sanctuary's inhabitants. Instead, he trailed after her, chatting the whole while.

"I saw that sail you put up the other day," he began, with an overly casual air. "Did Joy help you?"

"Um, no," said Sunlit, gathering her cleaning things.

"That doesn't sound like her."

"Well, it was late, and I didn't want to bother her. She's been doing the overnight feedings and guarding the pier."

"Uh huh. That *does* sound like you." Chip followed her to the desk, where she stowed one set of equipment before readying another. He insisted on carrying the bucket of fish. "When did you have time to do that?"

Sunlit's face flamed, so she kept it down. Did he know about the posters? Is that why he was asking? "I—I did it after I got back from eating on the pier with everybody. To be ready for sunrise, for the porpoises."

"Seems like a big job for one person," Chip commented.

Sunlit portioned out food into dishes very carefully before sneaking a glance at him, gauging how she could respond.

"And you can't tell me it wasn't," he added, with a conspiratorial grin, "because I happen to work on boats."

"I wasn't going to," Sunlit lied.

"Uh huh." As often happened, Chip did not sound convinced. He followed her toward the tanks, this time picking up the tray of dishes before she could say anything. Watching an old crab rather than her, speaking as though it was an afterthought, he said eventually, "Want me to take a look at it?"

Sunlit thought of the iffy knots along the mast, the only safeguard against a baby porpoise getting buried in sailcloth. It had held up so far, but according to the local weather forecast, a summer breeze would pick up in the next few days. She glanced up at Chip gratefully. "Would you?"

"Sure," he said, smiling easily. "But for the record, it would've been easier to be on hand when the thing went up, to do it right in the first place."

"But it would have been too late—or too early—and—" Sunlit gave up when Chip raised a dismissive hand. In fact, she'd seen the gesture often enough that it made her laugh and throw up her own hands. "I give up. You're just as bad as Joy. Fine, next time I'll ask you to do the weird off-hours task. Happy?"

"Better," Chip agreed, grinning. "Also, did your pocket just crinkle?"

Sunlit sighed a bone-deep sigh of defeat.

* * *

One difficult confession later, Sunlit sat on the pier as she watched Chip redo her rigging. It was nerve wracking. Not only did she feel bad about having done the rigging poorly in the first place, and terribly anxious about the letter they were now discussing, she was certain that at any moment Chip was going to slip and fall into the annex.

He was, predictably, so excited about the idea of Sunlit giving a lecture that he was practically bouncing. Even while climbing a mast.

"Think of all the things you could say!" He said, not for the first time.

"That's the problem," said Sunlit, miserably. "I'll probably get up there and not be able to say anything at all."

"Don't be silly. That might happen for a minute, at first, but then—"

"A minute!" Sunlit was horrified at the thought.

"—just think of it like a classroom full of Fishs," Chip went on. "You tell him about the Sanctuary all the time."

"He asks questions," Sunlit pointed out. "It's not a presentation."

"He'd probably love one though," Chip said, undeterred. "You could test it out on him. On all of us! We can make it a party!"

"I haven't decided I'm doing it. You can't tell anyone yet," Sunlit protested.

Chip finished his work on one end of the mast and slid down, cavalierly unaware of the way Zila was watching him. He paused there for a moment. "What is it that's really bugging you about this, Professor?"

"*Look* at me," Sunlit said, vaguely but with distinct discomfort. "I'm not really the kind of person to do one of these things. I can't even look after *myself*."

"Well, you can't tie knots," Chip agreed. "But that's fine. Nobody expects you to do everything—except maybe *you*."

Sunlit sighed. There was nothing for it, and if there was anyone she could admit her injury to, it was Chip. Huddled under her hat's shade, she pulled her hand from its glove and held it up. "It was kind of hard to tie knots like this."

Chip splashed over to the side of the boat, leaning up against the pier so that he could take a look. As he did, he whistled. (In the background, Zila whistled too. But whether he was agreeing with Chip's statement or complaining about all these intrusions, no one could tell.)

"That looks nasty," Chip said sympathetically.

Sunlit grimaced as she put her glove back on. "It was worse the day of. When we got Zila and Rainbow, I mean. I have ointments and things for it."

"So that's *after* two days of treatment?" Chip's ears went back, as if the very idea of such a persistent burn alarmed him. He himself was tanned to the point that sunburns gave him up as a lost cause.

"Not quite two days," Sunlit corrected, "but something like that, yes."

"So the sail's an even better idea than I knew when I brought it up."

Despite herself, Sunlit smiled a little. "That was my thought."

"I can see why you felt urgent about it." Chip mused for a moment. "But technically, this doesn't mean you're not qualified to give a lecture. You had a problem and you came up with an idea for solving it. It means you really *know* you're doing the right thing with your life, because you're so committed."

"Some might say too committed," Joy commented, announcing her presence before flopping onto the pier behind Sunlit, her whiskered nose and paws approaching the edge next to Sunlit's hip.

"You knew about it?" Sunlit had specifically *not* wanted to tell Joy because she knew what the otter would think.

Joy's nose twitched. "I didn't think you'd like to be told that you smell like medicine and coconut butter, kit."

Sunlit winced, but Chip chuckled. "I haven't noticed anything myself, but you would know, Joy. That said, shouldn't you be glad Sunlit's so committed? It worked out pretty well for you."

"I'd rather have a mussel every day than three mussels now and none later," Joy replied. When Sunlit and Chip just stared at her, she shook her head. "Landlubbers!"

"I got what you meant," Chip said, laughing now. "I've just never heard it put that way."

"Also, you eat way more than one or even three mussels a day," Sunlit had to point out.

"It's the thought that counts," Joy said primly.

"Not when it comes to mussels," Chip teased.

"And why," asked Joy, rising above the nonsense, "were we talking about Sunlit being too committed?"

Sunlit blanched. She didn't need *two* friends insisting she venture into public speaking.

Chip caught her eye and smiled. "Because as soon as I get the other end of this sail fixed, we're going over to see Pa. He's going to see that Sunlit gets an actual emergency kit," he added, to Sunlit's surprise and delight. "Let's make things go more smoothly next time, eh?"

12

A Sweet Fix

Ideally, one would have several different emergency kits for different rescue missions. Rescuing an injured dolphin, for example, is very different from recovering an invasive sprite. At the very least, an emergency kit must be portable, weigh as little as possible, and be as versatile as possible.

—*from* Standard Practices for a Safe & Sanitary Animal Medic

As Chip finished with the sail, Sunlit fed both porpoises and did her checks. Zila had taken to rubbing off his skin cream against the boat, whether accidentally or on purpose, she couldn't tell. She reapplied some, though she could see that it wasn't having much of an effect.

"I might try something else later," she whispered to him. "I know it probably feels weird to have this cream on you. Just be patient."

It was advice she herself found hard to follow. Chip's father, universally known as Pa, was something of a legend around Marine Sanctuary. After an injury years ago, he'd given up fishing and turned to carpentry—something he had a very handy talent for. Though he didn't come out to visit as often as Fish and Chip did, he'd provided many of the things they used every day—custom-built rope ladders and Joy's cleaning brush being two examples.

Sunlit was already creating lists in her head of things she could use in a go-bag.

"I wrote to Professor Lina for stay-wet towels and size-adjusting bottles," she told Chip as soon as the two of them set out. "But I really only asked her for the magical things. There's still *tons* of equipment I could use that's more commonplace."

"If Pa makes it, don't worry," Chip said, laughing. "It'll be way more robust than just 'commonplace.'"

Sunlit knew this from experience, and she was already excited.

From the Sanctuary, they headed south, going past Seaside's bustling new marina. While the beach and the boardwalk were home to tourists, the marina was home for fishing boats and business. Many of the fishers' actual homes were in a community just south of the marina, on the outskirts of town. There, snug cabins painted bright colors and decorated with cast-offs from sailing ships clustered along the dirt road, each striving for an ocean view. The landscape here went from natural harbor to rocky cliffs, but even the incline in the road wasn't enough to deter Sunlit and Chip. They made it to Chip's house in record time.

Pa was sitting on an old wooden bench outside the house,

watching the world go by. He nodded at Chip but smiled at Sunlit. The retired sailor looked very much like his son: tanned, white-eared, and tailed, but he wore his white hair slightly longer (and thinner, though not by choice). The main difference between them was in their movement—Pa was much more stiff, and much more careful, than Chip. He also tended to use far fewer words, having become used to his son doing most of the talking.

"How's the Sanctuary?" he asked Sunlit.

"Good," she answered.

"Full of porpoises," Chip added helpfully. "And look-ee-loos and even a vandal, I hear."

Sunlit came to a stop on the little garden path. "You heard about that?"

"From Fish, who got it from Ige," Chip explained before diving into the house.

Pa remained seated on his bench. "Comes by every morning to walk Fish to school."

"Oh, of course." Sunlit nodded: this had been a routine for a long time.

"These porpoises," Pa said, changing the subject. "Hear they were in an old truck."

Sunlit brightened. "An old fire truck, apparently. It was enormous, and most of it was an old barrel. Basically a traveling tank."

At that, Pa chuckled. "I know. Seen it myself, back in the day."

"Did you really?"

"Was a time when the fire chief down there was friend of a fellow sailor," Pa explained. "They're both long gone now. But I still remember the hullabaloo when the town bought it."

"Sunlit needs one," Chip announced, returning with three glasses clustered haphazardly in his hands.

"Not exactly, but it would be good to be better prepared to pick animals up," Sunlit corrected hastily. "We could help a lot more animals that way. Like when that colony of charmed sea stars got stranded below the marina—instead of having Chip ferry them one by one in his boat—"

"You could have just driven them straight out of the tide pool," Chip declared. He distributed the glasses to the little group, and Sunlit found her contained a very tasty iced mint tea.

"No," Sunlit said, although that *was* also a tempting option. "I meant, with a proper emergency kit, we could have erected a shelter there, on site. Or carried more than one at once," she conceded.

Pa took a long sip of his iced tea before looking up. "So," he said. "You're needing stakes, poles, rope, and canvas. Mallet too."

"Maybe it is a bigger project than I realized," Sunlit said, glancing with worried eyes at Chip.

Predictably, Chip shrugged it off with a grin. "So, rig it all up so that Joy can carry it. Or put it in one of those magical bags that makes things small."

"Do you have any idea how expensive those are?" Sunlit asked, both exasperated and amused.

"Well, we're here now, and let's see what we can do," Chip replied. "It's really all to do Pa a favor. He's been needing a new project, right, Pa?"

The man in question swallowed another draught of tea, then smiled. His eyes twinkled just like his son's. "Better take a look in the shed."

The three of them trooped through the small house and into the back yard, which boasted a lovingly tended vegetable garden and a small, ramshackle lean-to in one corner. Though they managed to squeeze into the shed and cluster around the dusty workbench, it was a tight fit.

"Ige and Fish've been tinkering," Pa said, as Sunlit glanced at the metal gears and various pieces of brass that took up space at the back of the shed. "My fingers're too old for it. But anything wood you need, I can do."

"Wood really would be best, since some magical creatures are sensitive to metal," Sunlit said immediately. "It'd just have to be sanded and polished smooth so no one gets hurt, that's all. Maybe we could treat some things with wax or charms if we need to. When doing rescues and field operations, the most important things are securing the animal and securing the space—as much as possible. We can't plan to *always* bring animals back to the Sanctuary, in case they're too big or too injured and we have to treat them on site. We got lucky with the porpoises—Zila's mobile, at least. But we also had basically no equipment, so moving forward we need to start from scratch . . ."

"Give him a minute," Chip laughed, as Pa reached for a nearby notebook smudged with sawdust. "I knew this would be good."

"It's the sort of thing every reference book has a list for," Sunlit said, a little embarrassed. "But I never studied it exactly, so it all kind of . . . slipped into the back of my mind."

Just like the lists had often been at the backs of her textbooks.

Chip gave her a meaningful glance. "So it's the sort of thing that would make a *good lecture*, is what you're saying."

"Where'd we leave off?" Pa, who had finally found a pencil,

asked.

"Not with lectures," Sunlit said, too quickly. "Um, let's see, I mean, rope. Like you said before, stakes and canvas and—what do you call them—poles. If it's not too much trouble," she added. Then., thinking of Rainbow, she couldn't help but add, "A barrel would be good. Maybe the whole thing would be in a barrel? A container for powdered foods and things. Maybe even some kind of portable screen . . ."

* * *

Hours later, Arietta and Fish found the three of them still excitedly poring over the little notebook, which was now full of sketches and several lists.

"Dinner, anyone?" Arietta asked, peering into the shed with a twinkle in her eye.

"*Everyone*, I think," Chip replied, leaping up. He grinned at Fish, who was also standing curiously at the door. "How about you? Are you hungry or did you eat too many cookies?"

"We made porpoise cookies," Fish said, distracted in his excitement. "With rainbow colors!"

"Awesome!" Chip moved out into the doorway to give Fish a high-five—something the little boy had just recently learned, and was clearly thrilled to enact.

Sunlit lifted her head, uncertain about this new publicity. But Fish was so excited, she decided to go along with it.

At her side, Pa stowed his notebook. "I'll get to work on it tomorrow," he assured her. To Arietta, he added, "Lost track of time. Hope we didn't put you out."

"Not at all," she said back, smiling. "The walk did me good. And it meant I could make sure a certain pair of messengers didn't eat everything I packed for you before it got to your door!"

Both Chip and Fish managed to look abashed, but only for about a second before they were racing each other into the house. Pa, Arietta, and Sunlit followed at a more leisurely pace.

"I've been experimenting with my pie crust recipe," she told them. "It's shepherd's pie tonight, and you'll have to tell me what you think."

"Nothing of yours is ever bad," Pa said.

The thought of veggies, potatoes, and buttery crust already had Sunlit's stomach rumbling. She had to agree. "All of your savory stuff is always perfect. Are you going to sell more lunch and dinner things at the bakery?"

"Oh, no, dearie. Some things, one likes to keep for oneself—and friends," Arietta said. Was it Sunlit's imagination, or did her gaze linger on Pa?

"One of Ebb's officers came by to ask if I'd seen anything about that vandalism," Arietta added, looking up at Sunlit. "I'm so sorry. I wish I had, but they were there when I first looked over at the Sanctuary this morning."

"It's not your fault," Sunlit said, again. She sighed. "If we're lucky, that'll be the end of it."

"You're not just lucky," Arietta told her before they joined the others in the kitchen. "You've got good food and good friends."

13

A True Story

> *Sometimes normal animals can have magic too! They can even become a whole new kind of animal. Charmed sea stars used to have no magic at all, but now they can navigate by the stars and travel very long distances! No one knows why.*
>
> —*from* The Children's Encyclopedia of Magical Water Creatures

After a wonderful night with friends, Sunlit woke more determined than ever to keep the Sanctuary and the porpoises in top shape. There were no new posters on the pier—perhaps because of an increased police force: a young officer she knew vaguely nodded at her as she went out to feed Rainbow. But those worries were soon forgotten, especially as she managed to convince Rainbow to bob around the outside of the tub in the annex. The little porpoise only moved in short spurts, but still, both Sunlit and Zila were thrilled. By the time Chip and Fish came by after school, Sunlit was feeling much like herself.

"Sunlit!" Fish called as he and Chip met her in the Sanctuary. "We saw a seal by the pier!"

"You did?" Sunlit was always interested in hearing about marine creature sightings, but this one made her wonder. Was it the same seal she had helped to free from the marina?

"Fish saw it, but I was too slow," Chip admitted. "So, are you ready to research an imp?"

"Oh—right." She'd forgotten about their errand, and felt a shiver of nervousness as she recalled it.

"What if I was an imp?" Fish asked.

"Do you like algae?" Chip replied, teasing him.

Fish's answer was decisive. "Yuck!"

Sunlit watched them and smiled. Even if she wasn't sure what exactly was going on with herself, she knew she could count on her friends. And how could this little adventure really go wrong?

When Joy came in and shooed them all out for her afternoon nap, the matter was quickly settled.

Seaside's bookstore, *Rachel's* bookstore, was the premier place in town for anything that might be written down. That was due mostly to a quirk of information-organization in Beyond: much like there was a system of witch schools and Witches, Beyond boasted a network of scholars. Each town usually had one, or a small group of them, who ran a bookstore /archive/library/building full of records, both historical and fictional. Though they were generally less flashy and less assuming than Witches, scholars were nonetheless dedicated to their role, often wearing long black robes as a sort of professional uniform.

Indeed, Rachel's outfit was the one uniform thing about her shop, which she had taken over from another scholar (in fact, a cousin) only a few years before. It was organized, of course, and completely functional, but still—eclectic. The shiplap walls and witty signs painted on old driftwood gave the place a nautical air (in case one forgot that the beach was only a few blocks away). Shelves of brightly-colored novels filled this first floor organically, while Rachel's office and town archives were located upstairs in the loft.

An old wind chime tinkled merrily as Sunlit, Chip, and Fish made their way inside. Sunlit did her best not to collapse into Chip's shadow.

"Up here if you need anything," Rachel called out, as usual. So far, so good.

Chip bounded up the stairs with Fish hot on his heels, the two of them already talking.

"Sunlit needs a good map of the area—"

"We found a water imp at school yesterday!"

"—one that shows water and things like that—"

"—it can blow spouts of water! Want to see?"

"No," Rachel said firmly, as Sunlit mounted the stairs behind her friends. When they'd fallen quiet, the bookseller went on in a more friendly manner, "That is, yes to maps. No to water. Books and water don't mix."

"We have a waterproof book at school," said Fish.

"That's very clever of your teacher. But—"

"And Sunlit gave me a book of marine animals," he added.

"You did?" Rachel smiled over Fish's head at Sunlit. Sunlit's heart stopped and then shuddered.

"Anyway, we're trying to re-home an imp," said Chip. "Just not this one," he added as an afterthought, teasing Fish. The little boy beamed up at him.

"Sure, no problem. I've got a couple different maps you could use," Rachel said, getting up from behind her desk. "You can even borrow them for free if you like. Just bring them back."

"That's really kind of you," said Chip.

"It's nothing." Rachel waved one hand, her black sleeve swinging in the air-conditioned, sunny loft. "Honestly, I'm just glad you're not here about the article."

Sunlit still had not found her voice, so it was Chip who caught on to this. "What article?"

"What—you mean you haven't seen it?" Rachel paused amid rows of low shelving units, and looked back at them with a difficult expression spreading across her face. Sunlit couldn't decipher it. Worried? Scared? Guilty?

"What article?" Fish echoed.

"In the newspaper this morning," Rachel answered, her manner becoming more vague. "Technically I think it was a letter to the editor. I thought—it's about—but maybe it's better if you don't—"

Below, the wind chimes tinkled again.

This time it was Officer Ebb's voice that rang out. "Rachel, you up there? We need to have a word."

* * *

Sunlit huddled in an armchair meant for perusing fiction. After the calm of her morning and the mayhem of her afternoon, her life felt *very* fictional, so it was appropriate. Chip, Rachel, Officer Ebb, and even Ige were in the main aisle just beyond her, and not even a solid bookcase laden with books could muffle their stressed conversation of *but what do we dos* and *who was it that sent it?s.*

Fish sat on her lap curiously studying the newspaper in her hands. Though he loved school, he was still working on his reading skills and mostly seemed interested in his set of encyclopedias on marine life—something Sunlit was grateful for in that moment.

For her own part, she couldn't help but read the offending letter again.

> *Dear Editor,*
>
> *It has come to our attention that vulnerable animals are being mistreated here in our own town. Two porpoises who need rest and real medical care are being kept at the beach as a sideshow attraction by someone who professes to care for them, but instead uses them only for her own gain. They haven't gotten any better under her care, and now in fact will probably get worse due to constant harassment and neglect!*
>
> *Some people simply aren't fit to run a Sanctuary of any kind. Some people are so two-faced and callous <u>they</u> are the real beasts.*
>
> *Sincerely,*
>
> *Concerned & Outraged in Seaside*

The newspaper was trembling. Actually, Sunlit's hands were trembling.

"Is it bad?" Fish asked. With his small fingers, he traced the outlines of each article.

"Somebody's pretty mad," Sunlit answered, her voice a harsh whisper. She cleared her throat. "It's not about you at all, though, just about me."

A strange blessing, but a blessing nonetheless. Some people in town had reacted badly to Fish's appearance last summer, and now Sunlit was fervently grateful that they'd never voiced their opinions in print—never written anything out, for a poor grown-up Fish to find in some archive or history book one day.

"But Rachel didn't write it," Fish ventured, looking up.

"No, no." Sunlit's stomach twisted. "She said she didn't know anything about it. Officer Ebb and Ige just wanted to talk to her because the people at the newspaper said that the letter came to them on bookstore stationery, they said."

Sunlit was losing track of her words, just a little. Her attention drifted. It certainly wasn't the kind of thing Rachel would write. But—

But also it wasn't *wrong*, exactly, was it? Just like the signs about her hating fun and irresponsibility—not wholly wrong . .
.

"Did Ige find it on the beach?"

"Hm?" Sunlit refocused on Fish, leaning her head down to rest it against his. "Um, he probably saw a newspaper there, maybe while he was at work. Or maybe someone told him. You see, there were also some signs saying some mean things yesterday, and Ige helped me take them down. So—maybe he figured they were connected," Sunlit realized. She'd only processed some of what her friends said when they'd first come in. She certainly wasn't listening to them now. It was overwhelming.

"So he got Ebb," said Fish, with a new learner's dedication to getting the facts straight.

"Officer Ebb," Sunlit corrected gently, shifting to kiss Fish's forehead. "Yes, maybe. But you shouldn't worry about it."

Fish's nose scrunched. "They sound worried though."

"Yeah." There were footsteps, too, on the other side of the bookcase, like someone was pacing. Probably Officer Ebb. Sunlit sighed. "But there's really nothing we can do about it."

"But what if you met the person who wrote it?" Fish asked simply.

Sunlit was struck by spine-chilling horror just at the thought. "I don't know. Why would I do that?"

"You'd say how you feel and then they'd say how they feel and then you say 'okay, I understand now' and you could give them a hug, if you like them and they like you," Fish informed her. "That's what Teacher says to do when your friend hurts your feelings."

"Huh. Well, I don't know if we're friends, me and the person who wrote this letter," said Sunlit. Actually, she was fairly certain that there was no chance in Beyond that they could be. The letter-writer sounded *awfully* mad. And what was even more bewildering was that they seemed to be mad about different things than the sign-writers had. Were there really so many things she had done wrong?

Fish considered her point, but it didn't seem to compute. In his world, everyone was either a friend or a friend waiting to happen. "You could let them see your water imp."

"Why?" Sunlit asked again, terrified by visions of crowds of angry writers and their opinions on minor magical creatures. *Inviting chaos! Cruel and unusual! Imp-risonment!*

"It's cool," Fish answered, with such authority that she almost believed him.

"Hey, you two." Chip emerged from around a bookcase, both frustration and softness mingling in the sigh in his voice. As he squatted down on his heels beside their armchair, Sunlit could see that he'd been pulling his hair in all directions. "Things got a little intense there. Sorry about that."

Sunlit wasn't sure what to say. *She'd* run away, but *Chip* was apologizing?

"Sunlit isn't sure how to be friends with the person who wrote the news," said Fish.

"No, I—uh—there's just a lot I don't know about it," Sunlit said, unable to fully defend or explain herself.

"You and everyone else," said Chip, smiling up at her with his warm brown eyes. "Rachel's headed upstairs to get a list of receipts for Ebb, for anyone who bought the stationery lately. Ige's about ready to go burn someone's house down."

Fish's eyes were big as saucers—

"Ah, not *really*, of course," Chip corrected. "Just, you know. Maybe stand outside and yell a bit."

"I don't yell," said the man himself, irritably, as he rounded the corner and joined them.

"You yell all the time," Chip retorted affectionately. "It's literally your job."

"My job is *safety*," Ige retorted. But, that said, he shifted on his heels and sighed heavily. "Something I don't seem to be very good at where the Sanctuary's concerned lately. I'm sorry, Sunlit."

"Did Chip tell you to apologize?" she asked, bewildered.

Chip beamed. "I might have."

Ige crossed his arms. "What's that supposed to mean?"

"Sorry, I—I didn't mean anything by it," Sunlit went on. "I just—it's okay. It's not like you are supposed to look out for the Sanctuary, you're supposed to look out for the beach. And nothing has actually happened yet . . ."

Chip and Ige exchanged a meaningful look. It went over her head, but Sunlit still caught it.

"Professor," said Chip, very gently, "Officer Ebb was bringing up some good points just now, about stalking and harassment, that sort of thing. Maybe you should talk to him about it."

"But what more could I tell him?" Sunlit asked, confused. At last, she dropped the newspaper to hold Fish closer.

"I think it's more like what he could tell you," Chip said. "Just to make sure you know that these things really are *something*."

"This is the sort of thing you need to head off right in the beginning," said Ige, with grim determination in his voice. "It's unacceptable. And I don't believe for a moment that no one else knows *anything* about what's going on."

It was a vague statement to Sunlit and Fish, but Chip interpreted his partner's words correctly. "You mean you're going to—?"

Ige nodded resolutely. "It's time to talk to Taiwo."

14

A Sailor's Yarn

Seaside has a long history of governance by town council. In fact, Seaside was the first town along the coast to set up an official town hall and regulated elections, which are held every two years. Town council members are paid a small fee for their time, but most run for office because they're devoted to their town. In fact, it's likely you'll meet one or more on the beach.

—*from* A Guide to Seaside (for the Discerning Tourist)

Of course, calling in city government wouldn't have been Sunlit's first choice. But since Ige and Taiwo were siblings, she supposed it wasn't *too* odd . . . Though she did feel a little uncomfortable, nonetheless. It seemed like so many people must be upset. What if Taiwo, in their capacity as town council person, decided the Sanctuary was just too much trouble after all?

"Don't be thinking the Sanctuary is too much trouble after all," said Officer Ebb.

Sunlit nearly walked into a lamp post. With her friends all busy on new errands, Ebb had offered to walk her back to the beach—something that perhaps wasn't as safe as it seemed it might be.

"I wasn't thinking that," she lied, poorly.

Officer Ebb chuckled. "You forget who was the very first person to meet you when you came to town."

Reminded of that time, and desperate to talk about something else, Sunlit asked suddenly, "Do you think I'd be a good person to give a lecture?"

"If it was anything to do with sea creatures, I'd say yes," Officer Ebb replied, his voice easy and fair. Though he strolled casually beside her, his blue eyes darted along the road: a child crying about a dropped sandwich, a couple of young tourists racing on bicycles, a small teal dog about to escape its leash. "In fact," he added after a moment, "that might be just what you need. Get up and talk at the next council meeting, give them a chance to really know about you and what the Sanctuary does."

"I couldn't," said Sunlit immediately.

"The meetings are all open to the public," Officer Ebb told her, his tone still mild. "Not that many show up. Unless there's something big going on. You could consider hosting a talk down on the boardwalk instead. Just need the proper permit, but it's very doable."

"No thanks," Sunlit said, alarmed to her core. The thought of giving a presentation to students she'd never see again was one thing; speaking in front of a crowd of people she then had to live among, and which she *knew* contained someone who hated her, was basically her current worst fear. She shook her head, her sunhat flapping. This attempt at distraction had been an utter bust. "Um, have you heard anything from Officer Emme and Last Stop?"

"About their old fire truck?" Ebb eyed her knowingly.

"I meant about the porpoises," Sunlit said hastily. "How the fireworks show got so out of hand, that sort of thing. And are there any porpoises lingering offshore, who might be waiting for Zila and Rainbow?"

"Zila and Rainbow, huh?" Officer Ebb tilted his head thought-fully, missing Sunlit's blush. "I haven't heard anything more. Except that they're *very* grateful you could take over. You might consider giving them a presentation, too. Maybe ask for a donation."

"Donation?"

"For the care of the porpoises," Ebb explained patiently. "Maybe get yourself a proper sun shade back there, replace that old sail."

"Is the old sail not allowed?" Sunlit now had a new worry: violating Seaside regulations about beautification and repurposing old things.

"It's fine," Officer Ebb said firmly. "I just brought it up as an example. I'm sure there's lots of uses you could put some extra money to."

Sunlit allowed herself to consider this. There *were* things about the Sanctuary that could use upgrading. Not to mention the true luxury of having enough extra money on hand to hire someone, maybe a student, who could watch the counter while Sunlit and Joy took care of things behind the scenes . . . Or even—

"Some kind of transport, maybe?" Officer Ebb suggested.

Sunlit blushed again. It occurred to her that maybe Officer Ebb was somehow a little psychic. Could coastal elves do that kind of thing? Maybe it was a skill he'd picked up from years of evaluating others' choices.

"I don't want to be ungrateful for the support Seaside has given us," she confessed in a small voice. "Without it, I don't think we'd be here now. Plus we do get money when people board their fish or purchase things. It seems rude to ask for more . . . Especially now, with—all the trouble."

"Every business needs a little more from time to time," said Officer Ebb. "Especially the new ones. I can tell you that much from watching the stalls on the boardwalk."

Sunlit had to concede that this made sense.

"Besides," added the kindly officer, "if you ask me, the services you're providing the town—the whole region now, maybe—could be worth more than what the council originally thought."

Sunlit could not disagree that healing animals was worthwhile. And—thinking back on Officer Emme, Sunlit could see even more of what Officer Ebb meant. It *was* difficult, finding a home for large or deep-sea creatures. And it could be very difficult for civilians even to know where to start with them—that much was clear.

Not to mention that there was a gap there, a place where someone could tell the civilians how to keep themselves and animals safe in the first place. How to not have fireworks so close to the water that they caused trouble, for instance. *Someone* might make presentations on that—not Sunlit, of course, but maybe . . . Joy?

Officer Ebb smiled at Sunlit as they came to a stop in front of Marine Sanctuary. "Keep an eye out, alright? Tell Joy the same.

If either of you sees anything, you let me know."

"Okay," Sunlit said, once more unable to disagree. "Wait—one other thing. Have they considered putting up a spell at the marina to keep out animals like the seal yesterday?"

"I recall some talk about it," Officer Ebb said thoughtfully, "but I think in the end they decided not to, on account of not being sure how it'd affect the animals already inside. Mussels, crabs, tiny things like that."

Sunlit was glad to hear this had been a consideration. She had, in fact, seen studies in her classes about marinas where the efforts to keep out large animals who could be in danger from the boats led to explosions of populations of small creatures, who then became pests. "There are adjustments that can be made. Certain new spells that have come out in the past few years—"

Ebb held up a hand. "Before you get too far, know that the person you should be talking to is Heather Del Sol, or anyone on town council. Don't give me that face," he added in a surprisingly fatherly tone. "You know I don't have any more control over that marina than you do. But this is the sort of thing that would make a fine presentation . . ." When Sunlit's face only increased in its displeasure, the officer laughed. "Think it over. For now, maybe take this chance to rest."

Sunlit exchanged a few more pleasantries, then ducked inside. The cool, dim light of the Sanctuary was an immediate relief.

"Oh good, you're back," said Joy, poking her nose in through the back door. "I just fed Rainbow. Zila came out to fish with me!"

"Did he really?" Sunlit paused, surprised. Of course they'd never made any attempt to confine the adult porpoise in the annex, but he'd been so dedicated to Rainbow that he'd never shown any interest in leaving before.

"Just for a bit. They don't talk to me like they do to you, of course, but I get the feeling he was ready for some exercise," Joy said briskly as she came in behind the counter.

Sunlit smiled at the news. She was used to Joy reminding her of her "gift" with animals, and let it slide without comment. "He'd have to really believe that Rainbow is safe here in order to do that."

"That or be sick of the fish from the sailors," Joy agreed cheerfully. "But they really do bring in very good food. Still, nothing beats catching it yourself. Speaking of, there's something for you, too."

"Oh?" Sunlit crossed the room to where Joy pointed, the sink and counter top that ran along the wall behind the main counter. There, perched a bit precariously, was a glass fishbowl with a little menagerie inside.

"The Seetons," Joy said by way of explanation.

"Of course. I forgot all about their vacation," Sunlit admitted. From its early days, the Sanctuary had become not only a hospital and rehab center but a boarding-house for aquatic creatures whose family were out of town. It gave them something extra to do at slow times, and brought a little income in as well— plus it was a fun chance to check in on some exotic pets. Sunlit was glad to see these, but she knew she was getting a little overwhelmed. "There's been so much going on."

"It never rains but it pours," Joy chirped. As a marine creature of mysterious origin, she prided herself whenever she could use a landlubber's turn of phrase in conversation.

"Something like that," Sunlit agreed. She surveyed the fish in the bowl: not only little striped zebra fish, but spotted giraffe fish with long trailing fins, one horned fish who kept to himself, and her favorite—a small pack of slow-moving, gray-scaled elephant fish. She loved looking after the Seetons' fish, purely for the chance to enjoy their themed collection. "Did you see them when they stopped by?"

"Yes, they got here right after you left," Joy said. "Paid upfront, as usual. I warned them the fish'd have to wait for you for food and room, but they were fine with that."

With all the grace and strength of a giant otter, Joy could do many things—but her paws were not quite dexterous enough that she felt comfortable dealing with the tanks and smaller creatures. That was solely Sunlit's job, which worked out just fine. Transferring the Seetons' fish to a tank along the wall where they could wait for their family to get back from vacation would be no trouble at all.

As she selected and prepped one of the tanks to house their "renters," as Joy often called them, Sunlit was aware that Joy's gaze was following her from behind the counter. While she filled up a pitcher from the freshwater sink, she decided she couldn't stand it any more, this feeling of being watched and judged. "Was there something else?"

"I saw a large seal hanging around the pier while Zila and I were out," Joy said innocently.

Sunlit had a feeling that this was not what her friend actually had on her mind. But she was grateful, somehow, for the distraction. "Fish saw one earlier today, too. I wonder if it might be the same one I examined yesterday—the one I told you about? I hope he hasn't developed some kind of habit of following the fishing boats. It could lead to more trouble, and he would be pretty hard to rescue, especially since we already have Zila and Rainbow here."

"Could be all that," Joy agreed. "Or maybe he just decided

he liked you."

"That doesn't seem likely," Sunlit replied as she carried her pitcher to the tank and began slowly filling it up.

"Why not?" asked Joy.

"*Why not!*" squawked Biscuit from the top of the tanks. Sunlit jumped, and water splashed everywhere—fortunately, it was meant to go into the tank eventually anyway. She hadn't registered Biscuit's presence at first. The bird cawed to himself in avian laughter.

"I meant it's just not very normal behavior," Sunlit told them, keeping her face averted as she went back to the sink for more water. The truth was, she was feeling quite distrustful of strangers—*any* strangers. And she knew Joy would figure that out eventually.

"Why not? Maybe he thinks you smell nice," said Joy, as though this was totally reasonable—which, for her, it was. Although her definition of smelling "nice" might not align with most land-dwelling folks'. "Maybe he liked the fish you gave him. Maybe he wants to thank you."

"I'm not the one who actually took down the nets," Sunlit said.

"Kit," Joy replied, "you don't have to do twice the work expected of you in order for someone to be pleased."

Sunlit focused on the fish menagerie, muttering rebelliously, "I'm not sure how much a seal would expect in the first place."

"You'd be surprised," said Joy, with a knowing air.

Sunlit sighed. She knew a losing argument with Joy when she got into one. "Well, next time we see him, we can ask him. Happy? For now, I have to feed these fish."

"*Feed Biscuit!*" squawked the parrot. Since he had his own trays of nuts and dried fruit distributed throughout the

Sanctuary and Sunlit's attic, everyone ignored his plea. Sunlit focused on settling the fish into the new tank one by one using a charmed scoop on a long handle.

"Speaking of food," Joy added, meaningfully.

"I haven't eaten since lunch," Sunlit admitted, watching the elephant fish swim happily, slowly, away from the scoop. "But I'll have a snack soon. Just let me get these folks in place first. And then—listen, I'm sorry I'm being weird about the seal. It's just—while we were at the bookstore—I have some things to tell you."

"Arietta came over with more food when she saw the paper, and she told me all about it," Joy replied. Sunlit relaxed, but only until the otter went on, "We can talk it over and make a plan while eating avocado toast and shrimp cookies."

15

A New Ally

> *The elephant fish, despite its name, is a small tropical variety, a favorite of dedicated fishkeepers. Though it gets along well with other species, it requires a delicately balanced ecosystem and low levels of noise. The trunk-like protrusion above its upper lip is actually an adapted fin.*
>
> —*from* Traverse's Guide to Marine Vertebrates, Invertebrates, and Magical Outliers

The cookies, it should be noted, were only *shaped* like shrimp.

Sunlit and Joy managed to have a restful afternoon, which turned into a comfortable evening despite the unsettling events of the day. In Joy's opinion, anyone who would write to the daily paper about Sunlit rather than come and say something to her face ought to be wholly ignored. Everyone, she pointed out, who had come out of curiosity about the porpoises had been very friendly, and had left in good spirits even though the porpoises weren't available to view. And that was the point, said Joy; how could anyone in their right mind think Sunlit was using the porpoises, when they'd been kept from the public since their arrival?

For her part, Sunlit still thought the letter-writer could pose a danger. She'd simply poured too much of herself into Marine Sanctuary to see it maligned . . .

. . . And yet, she knew Joy was right: there was a difference between *maligned* and actually *faltering.* Despite anything written about them, they were still doing what mattered: looking after the animals in their care.

Besides, Sunlit was used to Joy leading campaigns, and Joy was used to Sunlit protesting against them (unless an animal's health was at stake). And with the two of them sitting out on the pier, watching over Zila and Rainbow, no more angry signs or cruel letters appeared. Ige, Chip, and Fish did ride by in a memorable test of their modified dinghy, but because Ige was aboard, Chip didn't dare come too close to the pier or the beach. Which, given the speed at which they were traveling, was probably for the best.

In fact, the next morning dawned free and clear of threats or abuse as well. Joy was in good spirits after a night looking after Rainbow, and Sunlit had just finished feeding the various creatures in tanks when a knock came at the side door. She opened it on autopilot, expecting Chip or Ige, maybe with Fish in tow. Instead, she was met by a beaming politician.

But let us back up and try that first impression again. Taiwo Afolayan Rise was the best kind of politician: accessible, friendly, well-intentioned, determined, and more than all those things, a person first and foremost. Taiwo, who preferred the pronoun *they* (not uncommon amongst merfolk, to whom fluidity was a natural concept), had been one of Marine Sanctuary's first champions—and its most steadfast, at least as far as town council was concerned.

"Good, Sunlit, you're here," Taiwo enthused. Like Ige, they had deep brown skin and dark blue-purple scales covering their legs. But where their brother was often reserved, Taiwo was always in action, bright purple eyes alight. Shaking back long skinny braids decorated with beads, Taiwo tugged another person forward, saying, "Have you met Rei? I want you to meet Rei. Sunlit, Rei, here you are."

"Um, hello," said Sunlit, rather shyly. She had *heard* of Rei Rise, but that was it. He was that sort of person: the heir to one of the biggest companies in town, the family house on the bluff overlooking the beach, the whole deal. Suddenly, Sunlit was very aware that she probably smelled like shellfish.

If she did, though, Rei gave absolutely no indication that he'd noticed. In fact, he had the sort of presence that made one feel it was totally acceptable to smell like fish. He stood a little shorter than Taiwo, and much paler, though his elegantly tailored and colorful collared shirt matched Taiwo's floral dress—as did the gold ring each of them wore on their left hand. Rei's ring flashed as he swept a hand back over his short black hair, which was combed away from his face. "Hello, Sunlit," he said, in a soft voice that managed to be professional while also saying in an undertone, *please don't mind my spouse, as adorably excited as they may be.*

Sunlit's brain performed a full stop there. She'd known Taiwo was married to someone named Rei, of course, but she'd never had to actually put the dots together before.

Fortunately, Taiwo was still talking. "—and then I made

Ige tell us all about it, and we spent all evening coming up with ways to help, because I can't help but feel involved since I got you to buy the pier in the first place, and anyway what good is it to be influential people in Seaside if we don't use our influence?"

"Oh," said Sunlit, blinking. And then, "Oh! You didn't have to do that. Would you, um, like to come inside? It's not very fancy—"

"It's perfect, and absolutely *not* something anyone should be wasting time writing snarky letters about," Taiwo said, breezing inside with Rei along for the ride.

"You can't *tell* people what to write letters about, dear," he said as he came to rest against the counter. It must have been a very familiar refrain, because his deep brown eyes roamed the Sanctuary as he said it, and his expression was one of wonder rather than irritation.

"No, but we can certainly track them down and put some sense into them," said Taiwo. Turning back to Sunlit, they added, "Where's Joy?"

"Out fishing with Zila. A porpoise," Sunlit said, still confused. "The adult porpoise, from Last Stop. Anyway, they just went out to catch their breakfast. Um, sorry—did you say 'knock some sense into them'?"

"I did not," said Taiwo, emphatically, with a slightly guilty look at their spouse. "We're not going to do anything violent, just *talk* to them, that's all. And aside from that, Rei had something else to propose, we thought we ought to talk to you about it in person."

Sunlit looked at Rei. For as sheltered and academic as she could be, even *Sunlit* doubted that a town council representative and the most powerful business owner on the coast could really "just talk" to anyone. *Intimidate* seemed a little more the vibe of the moment. But she had to admit, she was curious.

"Firstly, we want to talk to you," Rei said kindly. Though his pose was entirely casual, his eyes on hers were intent. His features were naturally sharp. "There are several points which could be cleared up—"

"—starting with Last Stop," Taiwo concluded naturally. "You accepted two porpoises from there, yes?"

"Zila and Rainbow, an adult and a baby," Sunlit confirmed. Her voice wavered as she briefly wondered if she should have asked for permission first. But that was silly: Marine Sanctuary was *hers*, that had always been the agreement, and anyway both Taiwo and Rei were looking at her with complete benevolent attention. So she went on. "I didn't actually go as far as Last Stop, and I only spoke to Officer Emme from there. What happened was, I guess the officials in Last Stop realized something needed to be done for them, and tried to get Seaside Zoo to take them. But they don't have the space or the staff at the zoo for things like that, so they—at the zoo—they sent someone to Rachel to ask about Marine Sanctuary—"

"Did they know Rachel?" Rei asked, interested.

Sunlit ignored the pang in her heart. "Not exactly, I think, but they knew to try the bookstore as a place for local information. So she brought them to me, and then we went down with Chip in his boat to the zoo, where Zila and Rainbow were, in a big truck."

"They have a rescue truck?" Taiwo's glitter-painted nails fluttered in an appreciative gesture.

"Um, no, it was really an old fire truck, apparently," Sunlit said. "But it was a good idea, even though the drum had warmed up too much by then. Anyway I looked them over there and Officer Emme and everyone at the zoo was very clear that there was no space there or in Last Stop, so—"

"You took them," Taiwo concluded, as naturally as they had concluded for Rei. "Excellent. There's no problem with any of that."

"How were the porpoises injured?" Rei put in.

"A fireworks accident," Sunlit said, scrunching her nose in her frustration. "I really can't say any more than that. Officer Emme just kind of said that the magic had 'gotten loose.' But you can see how it's affected them. Zila's skin is green now, and the baby changes colors."

"Changes colors?" For a brief moment, Taiwo looked intrigued. Then they shook their head.

"Is it very bad?" Rei asked.

"Well—I'm not too sure," Sunlit admitted. "There's not a lot of research or treatments out there for their skin conditions, exactly. I've been trying what I can, but most of what I'm treating them for isn't the coloration, it's feeding and overcoming shock. The worst part is that one porpoise was lost—Officer Emme said it just disappeared. I think it must have been the baby's mother."

"That's awful," Taiwo said. "And for a moment it's just going to get worse, Sunlit, because this is where we come in. On town council, we've been hearing proposals for big development projects off and on for a long time—and a push to bring in more people with big displays, like the fireworks show Last Stop held."

"There are some business owners in town who think the answer to all their problems is *more*," Rei agreed quietly. "We see it all the time, but usually at a very low level."

"But this disaster at Last Stop stirred everyone up," Taiwo

continued. "Everybody has an opinion, some for it, some against it. And with the porpoises being here, Marine Sanctuary is higher profile, and so is the danger of all those projects, but the truth is, at the last meeting just a few days ago, we heard the biggest redevelopment proposal yet. Let's just say tensions are getting higher."

"You think that's why the signs and the letter came? Because the porpoises coming here reminded people that the Sanctuary is here?" Sunlit guessed. Taiwo made it very easy to put the pieces together, but Sunlit was still a little shocked by the possible connection.

"It's possible," Rei said, more cautiously, "but we should also consider that your Sanctuary might be a small piece in a larger scheme."

Sunlit was baffled by the idea. She stared at the two of them blankly. Over her shoulder, the water imp in its tank could be heard clinking its beads against the glass.

"Go on," Taiwo said encouragingly to Rei. "Consider it."

Rei smiled apologetically at Sunlit. "You'll have to forgive me—I'm not as good at *people* as Taiwo is. What I meant is, yesterday I also heard some complaints from one of my clients—complaints of harassment very similar to yours. So Taiwo suggested that we might benefit from sitting down and talking to them. All of us, to see if we could make a united front. That is, if you'd like to come?"

"To come?" Sunlit repeated, trying to will her heart back into place. "You want me to come along and talk too?"

"It'll make sense, you'll see, and you'll be stronger together," Taiwo said. "Rei, tell her who your client is."

Sunlit turned to Rei with wide eyes.

"The Zoo," he said, smiling his kind smile again.

Sunlit's breath caught. "Your client is—the *zoo*? What's your business do?"

Belatedly, she realized she ought to be ashamed for not knowing that already. But Rei just chuckled. "We started out doing imports and exports, but now we have a few niche branches, too. One of those is a specialized building firm. They're able to bring in rare materials for . . . unusual projects."

"The amazing exhibit houses," Sunlit breathed.

"Something like that," Rei said, with a modest blush. "What do you say to meeting with the Zoo directors this afternoon?"

Sunlit hesitated for only a moment. Though the notion of talking to people at Seaside Zoo filled her with nerves and other, less familiar emotions, she was starstruck by all these revelations and by the ease with which Taiwo and Rei talked about getting things done. "I'll do it," she promised. "Just let me tell Joy."

16

A Dark Turn

> *If you're looking for day trips out of Seaside, you can't do any better than Seaside Zoo and Aquarium. If you're relying on public transport, take the train to Last Stop and walk or ride the short distance to the Zoo. You'll want to spend all day there, adults and children alike, and catch one of their informational presentations or magical shows while you're there!*
>
> *—from* A Guide to Seaside (for the Discerning Tourist)

Had it not been for the fact that Rainbow still required frequent feedings and eager visitors were constantly walking by the pier, Joy would have convinced Sunlit to close the Sanctuary for the morning so that the otter could come along to the zoo, too. It was a circumstance Sunlit might come to regret.

But as she set out with Taiwo and Rei, Sunlit was admittedly enchanted. Just off the boardwalk, Rei had parked a small *hot air balloon*. Who traveled by hot air balloon? The Rises, apparently.

"It's a lot faster than you'd think," Rei told Sunlit as the three of them climbed into the basket. "I had a magic navigation spell put in."

"It's complete nonsense, really," said Taiwo fondly, tying up their braids in a long silk scarf. "But if you can't swim there, then I suppose flying there is second best!"

"With a first-best view," Rei added to Sunlit in an undertone.

Despite her utter unfamiliarity with the scene, she smiled.

The balloon's blue-and-purple expanse shot into the air, unfurling above them in a choreographed dance. More steadily, the basket began to lift as well. Sunlit only had a moment to think *oh no, is this* really *safe?* Before she found herself hovering above Seaside.

And by that point, she had to agree with Rei. The view was *amazing*.

There was the Sanctuary below her, small and serene, occupying its corner between the boardwalk and the marina like it had always belonged there. To the north was the beach, already full of colorful loungers and swimmers, and the lifeguard station, just barely propped above it all. The boardwalk was a crescent of sparkle and industry. Behind it, the town extended along haphazard dirt roads, clustered and clamorous and yet undeniably comfortable. Sunlit felt her chest swell at the realization that she *lived* there.

"The old family castle looks nice today," Taiwo said over her shoulder. They indicated the Rise manor house, gleaming in the sunlight atop the bluffs north of town, before grinning at Sunlit. "We'll have to have you over sometime. How have you still never been?"

Sunlit looked at the spacious grounds, the private dock, the multiple stories of windows and lattices and peaked slate roofs. Her first impulse was to say *why should I be at such a place?* But Taiwo had made it sound like the most natural thing in the world.

Rei spun the basket around with the ease of a practiced aviator, saving her from further contemplation.

"Should just take a few minutes," he said, speaking just over the wind and the rush of the warm air up the balloon. "Just a quick trip south-southeast."

"He loves this thing," Taiwo said, true affection in their voice.

Sunlit could see why. Though she had to hold her hat on her head as the balloon picked up speed, moving more purposefully than most hot air balloons she'd ever seen, it was still a magical feeling. Gliding above the marina, the neighborhood of sailors' cabins where Chip and Fish lived—and then above the expanse of jungle that surrounded the town. She hardly wanted it to end.

But they were soon at their destination, as promised. Lowering down *into* Seaside Zoo's parking lot was almost more amazing that walking into it from the jungle had been. Sunlit had a new appreciation for the building projects Rei's company had assisted with. The paths of the zoo, the houses and habitats, formed their own complete little world.

As the balloon touched down, Sunlit found she was actually *excited* for a meeting, for once.

A large orange tabby cat appeared on a nearby planter, waiting for them. "Rei, purrfect timing, as usual. We have much to—"

The cat paused, its yellow eyes narrowing into slits. Sunlit had to double-check before she understood that it was looking at *her*.

"Why would you bring that person here?" the cat hissed.

And just like the balloon behind her, Sunlit's excitement deflated.

* * *

It was like one of Sunlit's bad dreams was playing out, but in a new and idyllic setting.

They'd hustled into an office in a tree fort building to have what was turning out to be an *argument*, not a meeting. Happy children and animals could be heard outside the windows. Sunlit dearly wished she was with them.

Instead she sat in a wooden chair, hugging her arms around herself, as Rei stood behind her and Taiwo paced. The cat, whose name turned out to be Spot, sat on an old wooden desk across the room. Along the rounded walls, a host of other creatures had joined them: Geoff the griffin Sunlit recognized, of course, but there was also a two foot-tall red-skinned salamander, a child-sized rabbit which sat on its back paws and wore an apron, and a small polar bear. Mouse lingered in the shadows by the desk.

It was like being on trial in Wonderland.

Sunlit wanted to bury her face in her hands and never look up. But Taiwo's voice was too loud.

". . . And now not only are you telling us that you no longer want to hold a meeting simply because of one person involved, you're also *admitting* that *you wrote* that terrible letter to the Seaside editor, calling one of our town citizens a *beast*?"

Spot's tail flicked. "Technically, Mouse wrote it."

Mouse met Sunlit's horrified gaze frantically. "I didn't mean to! I was just writing what he told me to, it's part of the job, you know—"

"Which of you feels that way about Sunlit?" Taiwo demanded.

"We all do," Spot insisted. He seemed to be the leader of what was, Sunlit was slowly realizing, the Zoo's board of directors. With feeling, the cat added, "People may defame *us*, but the true monsters are the *humans* who will say one thing to your face and then—"

"Hold on," the rabbit interrupted. "Just because you feel so strongly, Spot, doesn't mean we all share your opinion!"

"I *knew* I shouldn't have written it!" Mouse fretted in the background.

"You weren't there when she picked up the porpoises," Geoff told the others. "Her behavior was despicable—"

"*What?*" Sunlit yelled so loud that both she and Rei jumped. "I haven't done anything to the porpoises! They're just fine!"

But then guilt struck her, because they weren't exactly *fine*. But still, they were *better*, right?

"It's not the porpoises that are the problem," the rabbit said, still trying to calm the others down.

"It most certainly is," Geoff argued. "To take them without a word and then to turn around and—"

"And *what?*" Taiwo prompted, when the zoo staff fell into silent fuming.

Silent fuming continued.

Rei cleared his throat. "Perhaps if you could lay out the events as you see them, clearly, we could understand."

Sunlit trembled. What would be said? Would it make Taiwo and Rei hate her as much as the zoo directors did?

"*I*'m not talking," Spot said, archly. "Seeing as no one here *values* my opinion."

The salamander spoke up in a wispy, dry voice laced with exasperation. "That's not what Wanda *said*, Spot."

"Let him think what he likes, as long as he doesn't insist we all have to, too," said the rabbit—Wanda.

"I don't see the use in going over it again," Geoff said, his beak in the air.

Everyone looked at the polar bear, who had yet to speak. The bear shrugged. "As long as the porpoises are looked after, what does any of it matter?"

Spot yowled and Geoff scratched at the floor impatiently. Before another argument could break out, Mouse jumped forward, claiming the floor.

"You see," he said, rather breathlessly addressing Sunlit, "they're awfully sensitive—I mean they have a right to be!" He corrected, over everyone's protest. "It's like this," he said, more calm and determined after his false start. "The Zoo is run by animals, right? Because back then a lot of them needed homes after leaving people who treated them badly, don't you know. For a long time they didn't have human-type people here at all. Then there was a spot of bother—just an expression, sorry," he said over his shoulder to the cat, before refocusing on Sunlit. "They found they *had* to deal with some local authorities, not just a few trusted business partners." At that his gaze flicked up to Rei, who bowed slightly over Sunlit's shoulder. "Well, dealing with authorities was a lot easier if there was a *person* for the authorities to meet, see, since that was what people expected, at least at the time. So last year they hired me."

Sunlit was too bewildered and mortified to even speak.

"What I mean is, just to be a sort of go-between, you know," Mouse said hurriedly. "I just bring it up to say, it's a sticky wicket still, sometimes, dealing with people, you see. Here at the Zoo, that is."

"Everyone can relate to *that*," Taiwo said.

"And we can appreciate why it might be especially difficult for the zoo directors," Rei added more professionally. "But how does this relate to Sunlit, Mouse?"

"Well—and I may be going out on a limb here, you see," Mouse said, twitching not unlike his namesake. "But I rather fancy that it was a huge relief at first, meeting Sunlit. I mean obviously it was a *great* relief for the porpoises to have a home, of course. But also a bit bracing to find another similar soul nearby, doing good turns for the animal folks, don't you know. Everyone was awfully glad right after we'd made the arrangements. So it was all a shock when the next morning we learned she'd put in a proposal to have the Zoo evicted, you know."

Sunlit stirred, croaking, "I never!"

"I agree, Sunlit's never even been to a town council meeting, let alone proposed something," Taiwo said. "Who told you she'd done that?"

The animals around the office shifted, looking at each other. Mouse seemed at a complete loss.

"It came in the mail," Spot said, slowly. "A copy of the proposal."

"Let me see," Taiwo demanded.

Spot looked at Rei, who nodded. "Taiwo would know what an official document would actually look like. It's a good idea."

Mouse crossed to the desk and drew the offending document from a drawer. As he took it to Taiwo, Geoff the griffin cleared his throat.

"I say," he began, awkwardly. "If it was all a misunderstanding of some kind—I feel responsible. I'm the one who had the letter idea in the first place. I brought the stationery back from the book shop. Rachel was kind enough to give me samples of everything, and I thought it might be in our best interest to maintain closer correspondence with Seaside. But if we were misled—"

"You were," Taiwo said with confidence, looking up from the paper in their hands. "This *is* a real proposal, but someone's left out all the lines where the identifying information goes and just handwritten a note about Sunlit at the bottom. That's not at all how we usually do things, but someone was clearly hoping you wouldn't know."

"As we did not," Wanda agreed quietly. "Sunlit Haven, we owe you an apology."

One by one, the animals around the circle nodded. Though Sunlit's breathing slowly returned to normal, her blush remained.

"We can do even better," Rei said gently when the silence had grown too long for Sunlit to bear. "Together, we can figure out how to face whoever sent you that proposal. Whoever it is, they've been harassing Sunlit too."

The zoo directors were clearly alarmed to hear this. Amid shiftings and murmurings, the polar bear leaned forward. "The porpoises are still alright?"

"They're recovering well," Sunlit said, her voice scratchy. But in the polar bear's concern and immediate relief, she did recognize a kindred soul. For this first time since they'd landed, she smiled.

17

A Bright Spot

We all want the road to be easy, especially when we're traveling. But sometimes, there's nothing for it. Sometimes you just have to face a challenge head-on.
—from I'm An Adventurer Here Myself

"So we have a common enemy," said Spot, all traces of contriteness gone. "That is where we have to focus now."

"I agree that we should learn more about what's going on, if it's part of some larger plan," Wanda said more temperately. She turned to Rei, her pink nose and whiskers twitching. "Do you know what's going on?"

"I don't, but I was very glad when you all reached out to me about Seaside," Rei began. "I'm happy to help, and I brought along my spouse, Taiwo, for their valuable insight into town politics. I also chose to invite Sunlit, for reasons you now understand."

The animals nodded, and Rei stepped out from behind Sunlit's chair to pace, much as Taiwo had, while he continued. "To begin, we can put the events in order. First: the heightened development in Last Stop, which has encouraged some kindred souls in Seaside, and which has already created some friction for you here at the Zoo. We were all content to keep our eye on this trend until the fireworks tragedy in Last Stop. Then, we had porpoises to rehabilitate, which led to the town of Last Stop, the Zoo, and Sunlit's Marine Sanctuary needing to work together."

Rei paused, looking at each audience member in turn. No one offered any contradiction. Sunlit felt she was seeing Rei for the first time.

"Next," he went on, "more personalized attacks began. The morning after the porpoises were re-homed, the town council in Seaside heard of new plans for development of the boardwalk, and rumors about the unfitness of the Sanctuary began to circulate. The next day, the Zoo received a letter meant to disconnect them from Sunlit. At the same time, Sunlit's Sanctuary suffered vandalism and protest signs. Those signs, by indicating that Sunlit was restricting progress and activity in Seaside, indirectly advocated for *more* development. Do I go too far in drawing that conclusion?"

Rei looked around, but again, no one disagreed.

Mouse, however, cleared his throat. "I say, Sunlit, did they really put signs up all over your place?"

"A travesty," Geoff declared. "Marine Sanctuary is charming and respectable."

Sunlit opened her mouth, then blushed again and forgot what she was going to say.

"They did, and it was," Taiwo agreed. "Obviously those of

us on town council can't run around condemning people all over the place, but everyone has opinions, and the right thing to do is *admit* them and talk about them in the proper forum, not write up signs like a coward."

"Honor in politics," Spot commented, clearly amused as he watched Taiwo speak.

"Since then, police patrols have increased and no direct incidents have occurred. Of course the letter was printed in the paper, but we know better than to take that seriously any more," Rei went on in a friendly manner, smiling first at his spouse and then at Sunlit. "Which means that in the past day, there have been no further direct attacks. Whoever it is was hoping you would turn on each other and save them the trouble, I suspect."

"Something we were only too quick to do," Wanda pointed out. Once more, she turned to Sunlit. "Again, Miss Haven, please accept our apologies."

"It's okay," Sunlit managed this time. "I understand. You felt betrayed, and threatened."

"As you must, too," the salamander beside Wanda rasped.

Sunlit nodded slowly, with the air of a confession. "I do. If anyone were to really try to take the Sanctuary away—"

"They won't get their hands on it," Taiwo said firmly.

"We could say that with more certainty if we knew who *they* were," Rei reminded them. "Does anyone have any ideas?"

Everyone was still looking at Sunlit. She shook her head; speaking felt like struggling to stay afloat. "I don't know," she managed. "But there *was* an incident—with another councilperson, Clementina—Ige was there."

"He thought it might just have been a coincidence," Taiwo said thoughtfully. "I agreed with him. Clementina might have been rude about your pier, but she hasn't brought forward anything to the council in a while. It's unusual, actually."

"But things *have* been suggested," Rei prompted.

"Oh, yes. A construction project, as you pointed out. And—"
Taiwo paused, and in that moment, the married couple exchanged a look full of meaning which no one else could interpret.

"Whoever it is, it doesn't matter," Spot said, with feline righteousness. "We'll stand by our Zoo."

"And your Sanctuary," the polar bear added kindly to Sunlit.

"Thank you," she said. "So will I."

* * *

"I say," said Mouse, when at last the meeting broke up and it was time to leave. "Sunlit, you wouldn't mind talking a minute, would you?"

Sunlit wavered. She would, truth be told. But Mouse had been very sincere in his apologies, and Rei and Taiwo were distracted, talking to Geoff and Spot. They hadn't gotten any farther in their discussions of the harassment, for now. There was no reason she couldn't stand a little distraction.

She turned so she was leaning against the railing of the little boardwalk that surrounded the treehouse. Taiwo and Rei were having their conversation on the ground below, having already descended the rope ladder. The rest of the zoo board was still conferring in quiet voices inside. Mouse looked, as usual, harmless and earnest. Sunlit sighed. "What is it?"

"Thanks," said Mouse, joining her at the rail. "Thanks awfully. I know it hasn't been a fair cop for you, not in the slightest. I just wanted to say I'm sorry again, you know. I should've known better."

Sunlit looked out, through the leafy canopy around them which shaded the zoo below. "It's alright. It's not like it was all your fault. Seems like Spot can be . . . opinionated."

"You don't know the half of it," Mouse said, grinning at her with relief in his face. He was so wholly *himself.* In that moment, Sunlit could see why Rachel might like him. She could even see how he might be a sweet partner for her. "Anyway," he said, recalling her from her thoughts, "that's not all I wanted to talk about. There's this delivery, you see, for the porpoises."

That got her attention. "Zila and Rainbow?"

"That's them," Mouse agreed. "It's like this. Back when we thought we'd be taking care of them, just for that morning or so until you came round, everyone was aflutter. One thing was where to house them, but how to treat them was another. We have our medics but nothing too special, none to hold a candle to *you*," he said, and he seemed to mean it. "So we wrote off to the sea witch, don't you know."

"You . . . what?" Sunlit's brow creased as she tried to understand.

"I know, we could have tried the town Witch," he went on. "That's what you're thinking, right? But Spot and the others didn't feel he was quite the right sort to trust, not when he'd been the *cause* of the trouble, according to all reports. That's the one in Last Stop, obviously—we've never had dealings with the Witch in Seaside, as far as *I* know. But we have had some business with the sea witch who lives in the caves around here. Something to do with polar bears and seals and goddesses of revenge and all that, see."

Now Sunlit understood even less. She was familiar with the concept of a town Witch—everyone was. She rarely bothered with Seaside's appointed magical practitioner, but that was beside the point. She'd never heard of any witch living in a cave. "Mouse, I don't *see* a word you're saying."

"You *could* think why shouldn't I do it," Mouse continued. "By 'I,' I mean me, not you, don't you know. Well anyway. I do have magic, as you saw. But only good for the odd gag or lift. *I* certainly wasn't going to try to cure the porpoises—healing was my worst subject, and that's saying something, take it from me."

This, Sunlit could catch hold of. "Okay, so you're saying that the zoo directors wanted something magical to help the porpoises at first?" That actually did make sense. Magical ailment, magical remedy. Things didn't *always* work out so neatly, but it was something she herself should probably look into.

"Wanted it, and got it too," Mouse replied. "Just in the post yesterday. If you trust the sea witch, that is."

Sunlit blinked. "Who is the sea witch? I've never heard about this."

"Ah, well, *that,* you should probably hear from someone who knows better than me," Mouse said, becoming rather more evasive. "Someone who's been around awhile. Maybe your police chief? I take it there's . . . some history. There usually is, you know, when a Witch goes off to become . . . well, a *witch,* don't you know. Off-grid. Unknown. Rogue."

Rogue. The word made Sunlit shiver, though the sun was high and bright above them. "But Spot and the others must trust this witch?"

"Enough to try, at least." Mouse shrugged. "I haven't opened the package, myself. Could be hen's teeth and hearts of innocents, for all I know."

"Tell me you are joking," said Sunlit, horrified.

Mouse looked abashed. "I am, a bit. Awful sense of humor. I only meant I haven't looked at it, so I wouldn't want to get your hopes up unduly."

"But . . . you do have it. Something that the witch sent in reply to a request for help, for the porpoises?" Sunlit thought it through.

"Came yesterday," Mouse confirmed. "But, ah, no one was too keen on sending it on to you at the time, see. Terrible shame, not least for the porpoises, but that's how it is."

A shame for the porpoises indeed! But at least he could admit it. Though she could not understand half of what he said, Sunlit was inclined more than ever to trust Mouse. "Are you telling me this now because I can have it?"

"You're sure you're game to take a look?" Mouse asked.

"Positive," said Sunlit. "I don't know if we'll use it, but if it—if it seems safe, then—"

How could she not try everything?

Mouse seemed to understand. "If you like, I'll take a glance at it over your shoulder before you go," he offered. "Might not be much use, but I could probably at least tell you if it's cursed or not."

18

A Tentative Treaty

All potions, charms, and magical conveniences must be tested thoroughly in safe conditions before they're used near or on patients. While magic is perfectly acceptable to use and can be a great boon to a rescuer in the right circumstances, if anything happens to go awry, the consequences can be unexpected and may quickly get out of hand.

—from Standard Practices for a Safe & Sanitary Animal Medic

She might feel a little warmer towards Mouse, but that did *not* mean that Sunlit was willing to trust her porpoises' safety to his opinion.

And that meant that she needed to research a witch . . . and most likely consult one.

As Taiwo and Rei's balloon touched down on the pier, Sunlit

was already thinking about her next steps. For the porpoises, of course. Taiwo, on the other hand, was still talking about the development drama between Last Stop and Seaside.

"... think I know who might have a stake in it, like I said," they were saying, even as Sunlit prepared to leave the balloon's basket. "I'll do a little digging of my own, you can be sure I'll keep you posted. If I can't find you I'll tell Ige at least. In the meantime how about you come to the next town meeting?"

"What?" Sunlit paused midstep, turning to look at Taiwo over her shoulder.

The merperson grinned. "You don't even know when it is."

"Don't tease her," Rei reprimanded his spouse from his position behind the steering wheel.

"I'm just teasing a *little*," Taiwo said, setting one hand on their hip. "You missed the plan earlier, Sunlit, so it's not your fault anyway. I'm going to call a special meeting for tomorrow night, to address the allegations on both sides. I already invited someone from the Zoo to come speak before we left, but it really makes the most sense for *you* to talk and share your side of things."

Sunlit's wide-eyed gaze of terror must have spoken eloquently, because Taiwo coughed slightly and added, "Or, you can delegate someone to speak for the Sanctuary. As long as your side gets heard, understand?"

"Okay," Sunlit said, nodding numbly. "Um, thanks for the ride. And for inviting me to the meeting," she added, glancing back at Rei. Her last impression was of both him and his spouse smiling encouragingly before she scuttled away.

There were people at the shore end of the pier again today, so Sunlit kept her head down. They were probably animal enthusiasts—one seemed to have a tail-shaped hat on—but even so, she didn't want to brave the attention. Aside from them, the Sanctuary and its pier were quiet. Both porpoises were resting in the shade as she passed them by. Then Sunlit skidded to a halt and took another look. *Both* porpoises were in the deeper section of the annex. Rainbow had left the tub and was floating next to Zila!

Sunlit was still staring down at the two of them as she became aware of Joy's steps behind her. When her nose was level with Sunlit's shoulder, the otter spoke.

"The baby started making a fuss after lunch," she said. "Zila and I helped her out. I thought you might like to see that!"

"I do," Sunlit agreed, though a little uncertainly. She had become so used to thinking of Rainbow as simply "the baby" that she was taken aback at first by Joy referring to her as "her" instead. But Joy was right, of course, as Joy so often was. Somehow, it almost made Sunlit feel jealous. Maybe, she thought, it was just guilt about having been gone all morning. So she turned to more practical considerations. "Neither of them wanted to leave the annex, though?"

"Seems Rainbow will float and hop but not actually swim," Joy confirmed. "And Zila didn't seem to want to go fishing once she was out."

"No, of course not. We're halfway there, then," Sunlit said, biting her lip as she watched the porpoises. "With Rainbow swimming at least. There's still their skin color—nothing I try makes much difference at all—but I got this package from Mouse, who got it from someone called the sea witch?"

"Interesting," said Joy, whiskers twitching as she considered the brown paper parcel in Sunlit's arms. "How was it at the Zoo?"

"Horrible." Sunlit shuddered. "Turns out they're the ones

who wrote the letter to the paper. But then not too bad by the end I guess. We're on the same page, they were just confused and thought I'd attacked *them*. They're worried about the porpoises too, but of course that means we have to protect the Sanctuary, and the Zoo, which means we have to go to town council and fight some big important developer and the people who put on the fireworks displays everybody seems to love, and on top of that I'm not sure this potion—or whatever it is—is actually safe, and so I have to look up whoever the sea witch is, which means I probably have to *visit* the town witch here, even though she was involved in all the trouble with Fish and I've basically ignored her for a year ever since the protective spells on the shop were renewed. And then there's lunch which I didn't eat and I know you will give me a hard time but also it will be Rainbow's feeding time soon and I don't want to ask you to keep watching them both, especially when there's a crowd here and you probably haven't gotten any peace. Plus there's the water imp which I promised Fish we could re-home today, even though I have to find out where, because it seems just fine although now it's probably developed some kind of attachment to the Sanctuary after being left too long and—"

"Stop," Joy insisted, shoving her cold nose into Sunlit's cheek. "Stop it. Stop borrowing trouble."

"I'm not borrowing trouble," Sunlit protested. "These are all *my* troubles! And yes, maybe I'm overly stressed, but I have reason!"

She found she was panting slightly. Everything she'd kept a tight lid on at the Zoo was leaking all over the place now.

"No," said Joy, very firmly. "Those aren't just *your troubles*. They're also your choices. All those last things you've said that you're stressed about is something you have chosen to do or to let happen. Kit, you were just at a public attraction in *very* good company. If you had mentioned lunch time, they would have made sure you had something to eat."

"I didn't *choose* for people to be angry about the Sanctuary," Sunlit protested.

Joy was not impressed. "But did you speak up for yourself when they got things wrong? And in your heart, did you choose to let it go or to let it fester?"

They both knew the answer to that, but Sunlit was on a roll now. "I didn't choose to be so bad at talking to people," she said sharply. "I didn't make myself this way. I didn't choose to have a skin condition so bad I can't even take care of a baby porpoise without second degree burns!"

"You sound just like that baby porpoise would," Joy retorted. "The point isn't whether you chose misfortune. The point is what you choose to do about it. Kit, the trouble is that you *focus* on troubles instead of on yourself."

"I—I—I don't have anything to say," Sunlit declared. "This is a waste of time. I have work to do. I have to go find the town Witch."

From the end of the pier where a crowd of porpoise-lovers were, apparently, listening in, a small voice said, "here!"

* * *

Seaside's favorite cafe was on the main street just behind the boardwalk, and it was always brimming with people. Lattes and teas enhanced with magical boosts or pretty sparkles and paper umbrellas never failed to draw in crowds, particularly when the ice cubes clinking in the drinks were part of the attraction— customers could choose herbed cubes, espresso, or fun animal shapes that didn't melt, leading to hours of playtime on the beach with crystalline creatures.

Sunlit did not notice that there were porpoise-shaped ice cubes in her drink and she did not notice that her iced black tea was, in fact, rainbow-colored. She was undoubtedly the only one in the place scowling.

"Hard not to be in a good mood when you have iced coffee. Or tea," said her companion. But her companion sounded distinctly uncertain and rather uncomfortable.

Sunlit didn't care in the slightest. Even in the best of circumstances, she didn't have a lot of time for Witches. Especially not at the moment, when she was currently responsible for magically-injured porpoises.

"I'll just, ah, take a look at that potion for you, will I?" asked Seaside's town Witch.

Reluctantly, Sunlit handed her parcel across the table. The Witch of Seaside—Tanja, to her friends—appeared to be an older woman with a matronly air, waves of gray hair coming down over her pink shoulders, and mottled gray-and-white rabbit-like ears rising from her head. She wasn't wearing robes or anything of the sort: unlike scholars, Witches had no official costume. Instead, she wore a distressed tank top bearing an ink drawing of porpoises over a floor-length, patchwork skirt in all colors. Her eyes were deep brown, large, and wrinkled at the corners, prone to sympathy, but she wasn't getting much to work with from Sunlit.

Aside from a potion bottle, of course. Tanja unwrapped the brown paper to reveal the sort of bottle that might be used to sell olive oil, except that it was full of a neon yellow solution. A paper tag had been tied to the neck of the bottle with rough twine and subsequently squished a dozen different ways. Tanja unfolded this carefully and squinted, holding it at a distance to read it. The bottle tipped perilously but even this did not get a reaction from Sunlit.

"'Pour into the porpoise pen with no more than . . . mmm, does that say quarts? . . . of water, leave to soak three hours,'" Tanja read out loud. She turned over the tag and continued. "'This is a standard detox potion. Don't come asking questions.' Well," she said in her normal voice, laughing a little, "that does sound like Clemency."

Sunlit shook herself. "The sea witch? You know them?"

"Her," Tanja corrected. "I only know *of* her, myself, but I've heard enough about her methods over the years."

"Enough to trust her?" Sunlit asked, getting to the point.

Tanja considered Sunlit, then returned her gaze to the bottle. For a moment her irises glowed orange and her hair lifted from her shoulders, but the moment soon passed. "For whether to trust Clemency, you'd have to ask Officer Ebb, I think. Like I said, I never met her. But I can tell you this is not a standard detox potion."

"It's not?" Sunlit sat up. Mouse had said it seemed fine, but what did Mouse know, anyway?

"Oh, it's a perfectly fine detox potion," Tanja said. "There's nothing wrong with it that *I* can see. But it's strong. Much, much stronger than anything most people would be able to make."

"Then that's probably a good thing." Sunlit hesitated. "Isn't there any way to test it before we try it?"

"I understand your concern for the porpoises," Tanja said, pushing the bottle back across the table, "but I'm afraid that's how magic works. There comes a point when you just have to trust it."

"Trust a mysterious bottle I didn't ask for," Sunlit amended, eyeing the thing.

"Trust the people who commissioned it. Trust me, looking at it for you. Trust the person who made it, if you like," Tanja corrected.

Sunlit winced. When she and Fish had arrived in Seaside separately the year before, Tanja had not made things easy. But that was long over now. And she *could* trust Mouse, too, whose opinion confirmed Tanja's. Possibly. If only it wasn't all so hard.

Tanja spent another long moment watching Sunlit from across the little table. She sipped her drink, an iced coffee with rosewater pearls. Then she said, "I'd almost forgotten how tough it can be, when you first start looking after people. Officially, I mean."

Though she said nothing, Sunlit glanced up to meet the older woman's eyes.

"It's a large part of my role, you know," Tanja told her, not unkindly. "Prescribing ointments for strange rashes, making spell pouches for imp infestations, brewing tinctures for common colds. Some people never think of the town Witch until they're sick or troubled. I always liked the puzzle of a new patient coming into my Hut to see me. It's when they walk away that's the hardest part. Will they take the medicine properly? Will they stay away from what made them sick?"

Sunlit's eyes widened and, without thinking, she nodded. She often had very similar worries about her charges. Rainbow and Zila not least of all. What if they decided to swim off, only to get caught in another wild display from Last Stop—or even Seaside?

"No matter how many times you tell them, sometimes it

just doesn't get through," Tanja went on, her eyes far away. "Sometimes talking just isn't enough. But you still have to know that you *did* enough. And when you've done all you can, you leave the rest to trust.

"The trick," she concluded, leaning in, "is to know that *you can't do it all.*"

Sunlit swallowed hard. Then she licked her dry lips and said, "Do you know where the water imps around here live?"

19

A Lonely Imp

<blockquote>

Some magical water animals live in springs. A spring is like a waterfall of water, but it's moving up! The water comes from deep underground and bubbles to the surface. Springs are very clean and sometimes very deep or even smelly. They're special places for animals to live. If you find one, be careful around it!

—*from* Children's Encyclopedia of Magical Water Creatures

</blockquote>

Not too much later, Sunlit was back at Marine Sanctuary with the borrowed map of town from Rachel and a hand-drawn map on a napkin from Tanja. Chip and Fish had arrived on their way home from school, right after she had. And now they clustered around the water imp's corner.

"But how do they go together?" Fish asked, holding both maps and waving them in front of each other, as though they'd click into place once they got near enough to the right position.

"One goes over the other," Chip said, squatting down and reaching over Fish's shoulder to take hold of the napkin.

Fish let his father take the napkin-map, but he still protested. "But then you can't read it."

"And they're not actually to scale. At least, I don't think Tanja's is," Sunlit said. She was assiduously not looking at the counter, where Joy was curled up grooming her tail.

"Both true," Chip said, chuckling. "Which is why it's good for you *I* came and not Ige. I'm great at maps. What you have to do at times like this," he continued, mostly to Fish, "is look for landmarks that are the same between the two maps. Like squiggles in the lines or other strange shapes. But remember one might be smaller than the other . . ."

As the two continued talking, plotting out where Tanja's depiction of water imp sightings lined up with a stream or pond, Sunlit stared at the imp itself. She was dying to ask about Rainbow's last feeding and whether the crowd had bothered the porpoises. But she was determined not to talk to Joy.

Not because she was mad or trying to punish her friend, exactly. But because the thought was so awkward—and painful. What could she say? *I still think you're blaming me for things I can't control, but also how is the porpoise I left in your care?* Just the thought sounded silly.

Not least because Sunlit *hated* admitting that things were out of her control.

But wasn't that exactly what Joy had been saying, somehow?

Sunlit shook her head.

"No?" Chip asked, glancing at her. "You don't think we should try Inkdrop Pond?"

"Uh," said Sunlit. "Sorry. Walk me through your reasoning,

again."

Fish took over, proudly showing her how the two maps both indicated a small body of water—one conveniently not too far from the schoolhouse.

"Pretty sure it's called Inkdrop because it's so deep and dark," Chip added, though he scratched thoughtfully at his ear and went on, "or maybe because one of the schoolkids was dumping ink in there . . . Decades ago," he amended, seeing the scandalized look on Sunlit's face. He went back to the map. "It's not as near to the school as the stream and this other pond, over there, but it lines up with some sightings from people walking on trails."

"Either way, we should go out there," she decided. She stood up too fast, her head spinning. "Fish, can you carry the imp like you did before? Then we'll . . . um . . . we'll be back soon."

That last part was said loudly, but not quite in Joy's direction.

"We'll be fine," Joy replied, nonetheless.

Fish and his bubble of water led the way out the side door. As they followed, Chip caught Sunlit's eye, but she frowned at him.

"Okay, not asking," he said. "We'll talk about something else. Did Ige tell you he talked to Taiwo last night?"

"Yes, and Taiwo and Rei showed up this morning," Sunlit said, reluctant to remember the encounter now. Even with the amazing balloon ride. "It's . . . it's been a long day."

"A long *few* days," Chip said. He patted Sunlit's shoulder. "Pa's already at work on your emergency barrel, if it makes you feel any better."

Sunlit couldn't decide what to say. On one hand, it did make her feel better. But on the other, she was struck by the fact that prepping a kit for picking up animals from farther afield was literally "borrowing trouble."

But it was also her job, so she still didn't understand Joy's point.

Fortunately, Chip was happy to walk along in silence. And it wasn't silent for long—Fish kept up a running commentary of how the imp was reacting to being in his bubble, what they'd talked about at school that day, and what kind of porpoise would be best to be. Fish's school was essentially year-round, with classes divided into four quarters and long breaks around seasonal holidays. They still got as much vacation time as any other school in Beyond, but it was broken up throughout the year. When the school had been set up, most of Seaside's residents worked in the fishing industry, which didn't take a break over the summer—so neither did the children. Though as many town residents now worked in tourism as in fishing, everyone had become accustomed to the school schedule.

Led by Fish and his chatter, they traversed the boardwalk and then cut through town, heading inland toward the school. Tourists and children of all varieties were still in the streets, despite the summer heat. Some looked curiously at Fish's bubble, but nobody stopped them, for which Sunlit was very grateful. She realized as she watched passersby that most of them probably had no idea who they were or what they were doing.

"You should tell them we're on important business," Fish informed her, when they were obliged to wait at a street crossing for a large group of cyclists to go by.

"You could have a Sanctuary-mobile," Chip suggested, his eyes gleaming.

Sunlit recalled Mouse and Rachel driving off in a Zoo-mobile and frowned again. "I'm sure we'll be fine. We're almost there."

The inland edge of town gave way to tangled jungle, much like the landscape around the Zoo. Beyond the playground at the school, trees covered in vines and leafy bushes with large bright flowers sprang out of the sandy ground. Chip led the way easily, taking them past an old swing set and a four-square court to a gap in the painted fence. After they'd squeezed through one by one, Sunlit almost thought they were stuck there between the jungle and the town—until Chip lifted one particularly weighty leaf and revealed a thin path.

"Stick close, now," he said, looking back at them with a wide grin. "And Fish? Herring mode. You *only* ever go here with a group, okay?"

Fish shuffled into position on his father's heels, close and personal like a schooling fish. "Herring stick together. Safety in numbers," he recited.

Sunlit couldn't help but smile at the way Chip had turned Fish's penchant for play-acting marine life into a useful teaching tool. Though Chip was perhaps more impulsive than Ige or Sunlit herself, he was a devoted father and, Sunlit thought privately, an excellent role model, on the whole. Not that she'd tell him that to his face: he'd be far too amused.

One by one they bent to pass under the leaf. Once it fell back into place behind them, the cheerful noise of town instantly ceased. The air was thick and green and rife with bird calls. The trees, however, were skinnier and more spread out than they'd looked from the outside. It was no trouble at all to follow the trail through the undergrowth until they came upon a brook, which ran alongside their path for several minutes. Then the path turned deeper into the jungle, up a little incline and from there down into a shady hollow. Here the trees clustered around a rocky pool no bigger than the drum Zila and Rainbow had been in. As Chip stepped to the side and the path opened up, Sunlit saw how this place could be a perfect habitat for a water imp.

"It's a spring," Sunlit said, looking into the depths of what could only be Inkdrop Pond. The water was clear around the edges, but that color deepened to teal and then quickly to black at the pool's center. Chip had his hand on Fish's shoulder, and Sunlit couldn't blame him. Judging by the rock outcropping and the still darkness of the water, this spring might as well have been coming up from the center of the world.

"Does it seem like a place the imp would want to be?" Chip asked.

"I wouldn't want to be an imp," Fish observed, looking with unusual trepidation at the watery pool. "It's too quiet here."

Sunlit hadn't realized it herself, but now that Fish had said something, she knew he was right. Though it *should* be the perfect spot, as Chip had said, there was something off about this place. It was unnerving, the more she focused on it. No more birds called overhead. No bugs or frogs were chirping. There wasn't even a wind.

"*Any port!*" squawked a shadow in a nearby tree.

Sunlit jumped like a frightened cat and almost fell into the pond—but just in time, Chip grabbed her. He and Fish looked startled, too. Her hand to her chest, Sunlit followed their gazes up to a smug mass of azure feathers. "Biscuit! What are you doing out here? You scared us!"

Biscuit fixed her with one beady eye. "*Any port in a storm!*"

"There's no storms here. You should be back at the Sanctuary," Sunlit protested. Rather predictably, the parrot did not respond to reproaches. Instead, he flew down and perched on her hat. That was probably the best place for him, given the circumstances.

Sunlit crossed her arms as she kept looking around. Why was Biscuit the only bird present? He couldn't have frightened everyone else off, could he?

"Fish," she said, thoughtfully, "what's the imp doing?"

"It's hard to keep hold of," the child replied. In the bubble between his hands, the water imp was rocketing back and forth like a balloon losing air through a tiny hole. It had seemed energetic before, but this was a completely new level, something approaching frantic.

"Try putting it into the water," Sunlit said. "Let's all take one step back and stand together, and—and see what happens."

Imps *were* magic, after all.

Fish had to lean forward to get his water bubble to move toward the pond—his control of his own unique magic was tentative, at best. Fortunately now Sunlit and Chip were both flanking him, holding him back. He lobbed the bubble the rest of the way.

The sphere of water audibly popped and splashed on the pond beneath it. For a moment, the imp seemed to have vanished, and Sunlit's heart sank. All four of them held their breath, rendering the clearing even quieter than it had been before.

And then there was a deep rumbling from within the pond. Bubbles began to surface on the water. The next thing she knew, Inkdrop Pond's waters were cascading in a small but very respectable water fountain.

"Cool!" said Fish.

"*Cool!*" Biscuit agreed, flapping his wings.

"Now what?" Chip asked.

Sunlit started scanning the jungle again. "Let's wait for just a moment."

She wasn't sure exactly what she was looking for. It was a good thing that Fish was happy watching the bubbling water, and Chip was patient. The trees around them remained silent . . .

. . . And then she noticed a dragonfly at the pond's edge.

"Whoa," Chip said, recoiling as a frog hopped past his sandaled feet.

Overhead an avian shadow swooped and receded. And then three or four more darted into the brush.

A swarm of unseeable bugs buzzed nearby, a dove cooed somewhere above them, and Sunlit sighed happily. "There. Doesn't it seem more *alive*, now?"

"Did the imp do that?" Fish's eyes were big as saucers.

"I don't know if it was the water imp exactly," Sunlit admitted. "Or maybe just that all these animals are drawn to the moving water. But I'd say you definitely found its home, Fish."

"So out here it's a *good* thing when the imp makes water jets," Chip commented, with a lopsided grin. "That's pretty neat, Professor."

"There's a lot of research on the way one species, or even one creature, can affect its environment and the species around it," Sunlit said. "One of my *actual* professors even compared it to . . . to a form of expression."

Fish was squatting on his heels, watching the frog. Chip's attention was equally divided between both of them, and fortunately he missed the little falter in Sunlit's speech. "So you knew the imp would do that?"

"Well," said Sunlit, recovering, "I didn't *know* it was going to happen, exactly, but it occurred to me that it might be possible, especially since deep springs often do have some movement in the water. The stillness seemed very unnatural. So then I—"

"Trust the magic!" Biscuit squawked.

Sunlit tilted her head back, though of course she couldn't see beyond her hat. "Biz, have you been following me around?"

She would have noticed if he had been at the cafe—wouldn't she? But then, Sunlit knew well that she had been preoccupied. And Biscuit was sneaky, for such a large and brightly-colored bird. Even when Joy was watching the doors of the Sanctuary, sometimes he would swoop out an open window in the attic. It had never been a problem because he only did it rarely, and then almost never went past the boardwalk—or wherever Sunlit happened to be.

In this case, in this moment, it felt a little like being haunted by a feathery conscience. A conscience that distinctly wanted her to push her boundaries.

"Trust the magic!" Biscuit squawked again.

"Where were you that you heard that today?" Chip asked, interested.

Sunlit shook her head ruefully. She'd explain it all, but first she'd need to get a little more comfortable. The imp and Inkdrop Pond were going to be fine; it was time for them to leave. "It's a long story. Come on, I'll tell you on the way back to the boardwalk. Does anyone else want dinner? I'm starving."

20

An Inky Word

Amongst all tropical fish, the zebra fish enjoys a special celebrity. This small, fast fish is always found in schools of twenty or more in the wild, though in captivity it can thrive in smaller groups of five to ten. Despite these numbers, it is rare to catch a glimpse of zebra fish in the wild—perhaps because they are so likely to spook. "If you see stripes, think eels, not zebra fish," as many a diver will tell you . . .
    —*from* Traverse's Guide to Marine Vertebrates, Invertebrates, and Magical Outliers

"So, I'm hanging on to the potion and I guess I'll ask Ebb the next time I see him," Sunlit concluded, licking salsa from her fork. "If he has a spare moment."

"Does anyone, ever?" Chip challenged teasingly. They sat across from one another on a picnic table at the northern end of the boardwalk, polishing off tacos. Fish had enough bean bits and fresh cheese smeared on his face to fill a whole new taco, but he seemed very happy.

"You do," Sunlit pointed out. She was in better spirits—though jealous of Chip's ability to wolf down his dinner. The burn on her hand was mostly healed, but not quite well enough to risk any amount of exposure. Thus she was eating finger food with fork and knife.

"That's where you're mistaken," Chip said. "I have no free time at all. It's all up to the boss." He leaned back, stretching his arm behind Fish, and then swept the boy into a bear hug that had him giggling.

Sunlit smiled as she watched them. "What do you think, Fish? Are you a good boss?"

"Everybody gets recess and two breaks," he informed her. "Plus pizza lunches once a week if you've been good!"

"Is that work rules or school rules?" Sunlit wondered, amused.

"Maybe it should be both," Chip suggested.

The setting sun cast a long shadow across their table as Ige strolled up. "Are you saying you reward your sailing crew with pizza?"

"No," Chip answered, looking up. "They prefer hardtack and cider."

Sunlit choked on her last bite of taco, laughing as she slid over to make room for Ige. Biscuit, at the other end of the table, was consumed with his basket of street corn and opted to ignore the mayhem.

"None of you look like you're working very hard," Ige observed.

"We re-honed the imp!" Fish informed him, leaning one

grubby hand over the table for a high-five.

"Re-homed," Sunlit explained, leaning back so Ige could give Fish the reward he deserved. "Fish and Chip found out where the water imp was from, and we just got back from taking it into the jungle."

"Into the jungle?" Ige gave Chip a look that was very much *what trouble are you getting Fish into now?*.

"Only a *little* bit into the jungle," Chip replied with his most innocent smile. "You should have seen it. It was like magic, the way Sunlit figured it out."

"The imp *is* magic," Sunlit corrected, embarrassed. "And it turns out it was very connected to its environment, is all."

The corner of Ige's mouth twitched up as he turned to her. "Not unlike the rest of us, then."

"You've been talking to Joy," Sunlit accused him, making a face.

"No, but I *have* been hearing rumors on the beach all afternoon."

"I guess if those are the worst rumors about the Sanctuary that you're hearing, it's not as bad as it could be." Sunlit sighed, rubbing her gloved hands over her face. "I should get back. Joy hasn't had any breaks since morning."

"Joy knows how to take breaks while she's working," Chip said.

"What he means is, she's good at pacing herself," Ige interpreted.

Chip was not to be outdone. "That's what I said, isn't it? Like how otters sleep for a little while, then do things, then sleep—"

"That's just napping," Ige interrupted.

"I could be an otter," Fish mused.

Normally Sunlit would have been more amused by their

discussion, but there was a pit in the bottom of her stomach. Even if they had a point—and they most likely *did*; Joy was very good at knowing her limits—it still didn't sit well knowing she hadn't even given Joy the option to get out.

Biscuit finished his corn and looked up. "*Borrowing trouble!*"

"Ugh." Sunlit began collecting her utensils to return to the taco booth.

"Hey." Ige stopped her, just for a moment. "Remember, the good thing about Joy is she can just *tell* you."

Sunlit frowned. "About breaks?"

"About whatever it is you're worrying about. Unlike the water imp and all the rest of the animals you have that never talk. You can just ask her. You don't have to puzzle it out."

Sunlit glanced over at Chip and Fish, who nodded. She doubted Fish knew what they were talking about, exactly, but everyone looked supportive nonetheless.

"Fine, I know," she said, giving in. "I'm going."

***

Biscuit swooped in through the open half-door before Sunlit could enter the Sanctuary. She trailed behind him, having to open the lower portion of the door for herself. He ruined her entrance . . . although what was she hoping to do, sneak up on Joy?

The otter was stretched out across the shop floor on her back, still damp and smelling salty, playing with an old buoy she'd found in the water.

"*Red sky in the morning,*" Biscuit squawked before alighting on the counter.

"If he poops over there I'm not cleaning it up," Joy said,

glancing at Sunlit.

"No, I know, I'll do it," she said automatically. Then she paused. "You do a lot around here. Especially today."

Joy shifted so she was leaning on her side facing Sunlit, essentially cuddling her buoy under her arm. "Do I look like that's a problem?"

She looked more like a bathing beauty than an employee. Sunlit had to chuckle, if nervously. "No, I'm just saying . . . I appreciate it."

"I knew what I was getting into when I stayed on here," Joy said in a softer, though still matter-of-fact, tone. "I'm not one to complain about work. I like having something to do."

"I'm not trying to—I don't—are you saying I was complaining about work earlier?"

Being covered in lush brown fur, Joy couldn't exactly raise an eyebrow. But she stared patiently at Sunlit nevertheless.

Sunlit swallowed, leaning back against the heavy divider that partitioned her exam room off from the main floor. It scooted back a little from her weight and she stood back up abruptly, wrapping her arms around herself. "I wasn't complaining about my actual work. Not what I've chosen to do."

"Landlubbers talk a lot," Joy remarked, an abrupt non sequitur until she continued, "It's a different kind of life, when you're underwater. You have to choose where you're going or you'll get swept along with the current. Everybody in the sea knows this without talking about it. Landlubbers talk but don't seem to get it. Sometimes by not choosing, you're making a choice. Sometimes your habits are making a choice for you and you're just getting swept along."

Sunlit's gaze drifted guiltily until she spied that bright yellow bottle on the shelf behind the counter. Joy must have tidied up earlier. Seeing the faint glow, worrying what it could mean for the porpoises and remembering Tanja's words, Sunlit began to understand Joy's point. "Like choosing *not* to trust in magic."

"Kit," said Joy, very gently, "sometimes your habit is not to trust anything at all."

"Sometimes that's a good thing." Sunlit turned back, her eyes suddenly swimming with tears. "I have to be careful. I can't make anything worse."

"Careful can be good," Joy agreed, "but what if you trusted yourself to make the best decision and to handle the outcome, whatever it is?"

Words piled up in Sunlit's throat like sticks behind a dam. "You said once I have to trust my friends."

"And that's true, but if someone's attacking you directly, you have to let yourself do *something*," Joy said. "Make any choice. It doesn't matter. Anything's better than letting it crush you."

"Joy," Sunlit said, as the dam finally broke, "I just feel so *small!*"

She collapsed into the giant otter's soft fur, wrapping her arms around Joy's neck. Joy pressed her whiskers against Sunlit's back, pulling her into an odd but profound hug.

"Oh, kit," Joy whispered. "You *are* so very little and young. But you're also so very, very big. So much more powerful than you know."

You can choose. She didn't have to say it again; the words hung in the air. The more Sunlit cried out her frustration, hurt, and fear, the more she could feel it. The misunderstanding at the zoo, the malice on town council, even the fight with Joy: none of it mattered as much as this moment. And in this moment, she was beginning to see her way forward. A path not to wherever the current might take her, but to a place she *wanted* to be.

She wanted to be stronger than this. She wanted to be the way Joy saw her.

"I'm sorry I didn't understand what you were saying," Sunlit said, pulling back to sit on her heels, wiping at her eyes. "I thought you were telling me everything was my fault."

"I'm sorry I lost my temper," Joy returned. "I was trying to tell you that it's not your fault and that therefore, you don't have to worry so much about it all. You just have to pick how to respond."

"Yeah. Taiwo wants me to talk to the town," Sunlit confessed, sniffing. "They think that will disprove the rumors and—and make people realize the Sanctuary is more important than some big development."

"Do you trust Taiwo?" Joy asked.

Sunlit nodded. "I know it's a good idea. I know they're right. I just—" she hesitated. Was she going to pick small Sunlit, a miserable and confining but familiar and safe space? Or was she going to try being this big Sunlit that Joy and all her other friends seemed to see? Even if it was the right thing to do, how could she do it if she'd never tried before?

"I guess I'll just have to do my best," she said very quietly, looking down at her hands.

Joy touched her nose to Sunlit's forehead in a whiskery kiss. "Your best is going to be amazing. It's already what keeps this place alive."

* * *

Sunlit slept deeply that night, curled up under her blankets. Her dreams were full of water and waves. She woke up to a fresh morning with renewed determination to see her choice through . . .

. . . and she also woke up to a new revelation.

It came in the form of Rei, who was sitting on the bench outside the Sanctuary when Sunlit let herself out to check the pier. Joy was snoring behind the gate and the sun was barely rising over the town to caress the water's edge.

Sunlit had to blink several times to make sure her eyes had not deceived her.

"Coffee?" Rei asked, holding out a ceramic to-go cup. He looked a bit more ragged than he had the day before; in fact, rather than his colorful business attire, he was wearing a dark long-sleeved shirt and black trousers, like a high-class thief. His short hair was clearly uncombed and his own coffee mug was lying on its side, apparently empty. And yet there was something distinctly triumphant about him.

"Thanks," Sunlit said instinctively, reaching out for the cup. She often didn't like coffee, but in this case it seemed warranted. "Um . . . not that you're not welcome, but . . . what are you doing here? Is something wrong?"

"Blame Taiwo," said Rei, with matter-of-fact affection. "They set us up to it. Themself, Ige, and me. We took turns keeping watch."

Sunlit blinked again. "Keeping . . . watch?"

"Yes. I took the morning shift thinking I'd go in to work right afterward, but I wanted to make sure I saw you first. Sunlit," Rei said, "I saw something."

"You kept watch here?" Sunlit asked. "On the pier, I mean?"

"Waiting for the vandals," Rei confirmed.

"And you—you *saw* them?"

"I did," Rei said, and it occurred to Sunlit that the way his teeth glinted when he grinned in that particular fashion was rather more predatory than businesslike. "And between you and me, I gave them quite a fright."

Sunlit gulped. "Um—but who were they? What were they doing?"

"They were hoping to spray-paint your Sanctuary," Rei said. "They dropped their paint, and I saved it for Officer Ebb. They left in a hurry, but I got a very clear look. It was definitely employees of Del Sol Developments."

21

A Special Delivery

The cliffs outside of Seaside boast many caves. In fact, there are even caverns under parts of the town in some places. However, it's best not to explore them without a guided tour. Some are privately owned, and others are rumored to be home to ancient secrets and very odd creatures who prefer to roam in the dark.

—from A Guide to Seaside (for the Discerning Tourist)

Sunlit hadn't even thought of Del Sol. Taiwo had, clearly, because Rei didn't seem surprised: it seemed the couple had discussed this as a possible outcome.

While Sunlit was still wrapping her mind around this, a police patrol came by. The junior police officer took one look at Rei Rise and was already offering to run for Officer Ebb before Rei had even explained his stakeout. He was insistent that the officer not *run*, however, and promised that he'd wait patiently. "It's early still," he explained to Sunlit, as the police officer speed-walked away. "Do you need to see to the animals? Feel free to go about your work. I'll just be here."

Sunlit appreciated that. There was always seeing to the animals that she could do, especially when human matters were threatening to get complicated again. Speaking up at town council where an audience probably didn't like her was one thing. But speaking up *knowing* that she was going against the biggest developer in town? Sunlit could feel the nerves already.

During their conversation with the officer, Joy had begun to wake. The giant otter yawned as Sunlit reemerged on the pier, a fresh porpoise bottle in hand. Rather hastily, she introduced Rei and Joy. She could have gotten to the porpoises via the back door, but she supposed it was good to make sure everyone knew each other—and knew not to fight.

The normally chatty Joy opted not to focus on the newcomer, though. As soon as Sunlit unlocked the gate to let herself through, Joy was following her to the annex.

"He's the one who knew the board of the Zoo?" Joy asked, not entirely quietly.

"Yeah. He's Taiwo's spouse." Sunlit scanned the sunken boat, noting Zila in the sliver of morning sunlight at the far side and Rainbow resting against her tub in the shallows. Sunlit wondered if she'd been trying to get back into it.

"I put Rainbow in the tub but then she got out overnight," Joy reported, anticipating the question. In a lower voice, she added, "Do you trust Rei?"

Sunlit paused in clambering down the rope ladder from the pier, bottle in one arm. Though she hadn't actually thought about this directly, she *had* left the gate unlocked right next to him, so subconsciously she'd clearly already made a choice. "Yes? Why?"

"Nothing." Joy's nose twitched. "He smells like . . . what are those small predators in the forest with bushy tails?"

There was too much going on for guessing games. Sunlit let herself down into the water and crossed to Rainbow, her brow furrowed. "How do you know what they smell like if you don't know what they're called?"

"I know what they're called," Joy protested. "I just forgot. They're red."

"Foxes?" Sunlit pursed her lips. "Those are bigger than most otters, you know."

"Normal otters," Joy corrected cheerfully. "Yes, that's it. He smells like a fox."

As Rainbow nestled into her lap and began feeding, Sunlit couldn't help but recall that odd glint in Rei's expression earlier. But she shrugged it off. She'd seen both Taiwo and Rei stand up for her yesterday, in a very real way, and it didn't usually matter what people smelled like. It was just one of the ways Joy seemed to keep all the land–dwelling residents of Seaside separate in her mind.

"You don't smell like herbs today," Joy added, taking up a comfy position on the pier to wash her ears with her paws.

Case in point, Sunlit told herself, smiling faintly. "I skipped the ointment this morning. The skin is basically healed, it's just especially tender and vulnerable. I'm keeping the glove on at all times for now." It felt strange to be talking about her own care. She ran one hand over Rainbow's back. "Rainbow and Zila have recovered from all the dryness and rough skin patches, but the creams haven't done much. The next step, I suppose, is to try the potion." She paused, and dearly wished she could ask the porpoises if they wanted to go through with the treatment. Did they care that they were different from other porpoises now? Was it worth taking the risk?

Once again, Joy seemed to intuit her thoughts. "Zila does alright fishing, since his head's the darkest green. He can sort of blend in and sneak up on fish. But baby Rainbow there . . ."

"You're right. There's no way color patterns like that won't affect her feeding. Once you're grown up and getting your own food," she added to Rainbow affectionately. The baby porpoise nosed at the bottle, now empty. From the deeper side of the annex, Zila whistled.

"Do you ever wonder what he's saying?" Joy asked.

"All the time," Sunlit confirmed. But there was no way to know, so she fell back on an earlier thought. "Did *you* wonder what Rei's doing here?"

"I heard enough about police officers to know I'll find out soon," Joy said. She went still, and then glanced toward the Sanctuary. "Speaking of, I hear him coming now."

"Alright. I think we're good here," Sunlit said, lifting the bottle from Rainbow. For a moment, the baby porpoise strained after it.

"Huh." Heartened, Sunlit decided to try an experiment. She pushed Rainbow off her lap—gently, of course. The porpoise floundered a little and gave her a baleful stare before lurching towards Zila, who immediately offered conciliatory cuddles.

It wasn't swimming, exactly. But it wasn't sitting in a tub overwhelmed with exhaustion, either.

"Whenever I try to do that with you, you get very upset," Joy commented.

Sunlit knew her well enough to know she was teasing, and

she met her friend's gaze with a smile. "I'm the vet here. It's different."

Both Joy and Sunlit were laughing when Rei, with Officer Ebb in tow, joined them.

"We thought it was best to talk farther away from prying ears," Rei said. When Sunlit followed his glance, she saw that they did already have a few curious onlookers lingering by the gate. "I hope you don't mind?"

"It's fine," Sunlit agreed. "I'll join you up there, just give me a minute."

She stood and made her way to the pier, trying to splash as little as possible. But it didn't matter now the way it would have when the porpoises first arrived. Both Zila and Rainbow were accustomed to the routine—and they both were more relaxed, too. Despite everything else going on, that thought carried Sunlit, lightening her mood. And when she stood on the pier facing Ebb and Rei, dripping, the morning sun already drying out her long pants, she didn't feel quite as confused as she had before.

"Somebody start from the beginning, now that we're all here," Officer Ebb suggested. He raised one eyebrow at Rei, challenging the business owner to explain his presence.

And explain he did, with the same calm and flair for expression Sunlit had noticed yesterday. "Ige came to Taiwo about the troubles Marine Sanctuary has been having, and Taiwo looped me in, as well. As it happens, I work closely with the Zoo, and I knew they were anxious about similar things happening to them. Taiwo, Sunlit, and I went to meet with the zoo directors yesterday, and we came away convinced that there is someone in Seaside targeting both the Zoo and the Sanctuary. And while we were aware of your own investigations, of course," he said, bowing his head to Officer Ebb, who was both taller and older but took the gesture with amused grace, "we still felt that there was, ah, something extra we could do. So we agreed—that is, Taiwo, Ige, and I; Sunlit didn't know at the time—we agreed to keep active watch of the Sanctuary all night. This morning just before dawn, I encountered two figures carrying spray paint, who ran when they saw me. I can however identify them as employees of Del Sol."

Officer Ebb shifted on his heels, considering this. "Eyewitness testimony is notoriously unreliable."

"My sight is very good in the dark," Rei said.

"I'm sure it is," Ebb agreed, and for a moment the two seemed to share an understanding that eluded Sunlit. "And I'm not saying I don't trust your word, mind. But I need to be certain before I bring anybody in."

Sunlit sputtered. "Is—is that really the next step?"

Officer Ebb's head swiveled to her. "What would you like to propose?"

"Um—I don't know—I just thought," she said, gathering her breath, "I just thought it was bad enough to know who might be behind all this."

"We don't know for sure until I've done some questioning," Officer Ebb said patiently. He glanced over Sunlit's shoulder at Joy. "Did you happen to notice anything?"

The otter shook her head, her whiskers brushing past Sunlit's hat. "I was on the pier and I'd talked to Ige last evening about their plan, but we agreed my presence was off-putting enough without me keeping watch. When I'm on dry land I tend to sleep very deeply.

"But," she added, leaning forward, "that can you have smells like dirt."

"Does it?" That must have meant more to Officer Ebb than to Sunlit, because he smirked. Using his handkerchief as a barrier, he was carrying the paint canister Rei had found. "Alright, you've given me enough to follow up on, at least. No words were exchanged?" He glanced at Rei for confirmation.

Rei, too, smirked a little. "They ran off *very* fast."

"That's all I want," Sunlit said suddenly. When everyone looked back to her, she faltered but explained, "I just want them to stop. That's all."

"I appreciate that," Officer Ebb said slowly. "But what they've done is still criminal. The town could choose to prosecute them for disturbance of the peace."

Sunlit glanced at Rei and then at Joy, uncertain what to say.

"We can leave those kinds of decisions for later," Officer Ebb continued kindly. "The investigation will take time, even with this new development. In the meantime, I believe you have a meeting to attend tonight."

"Will you be there?" Rei asked him.

The officer nodded. "We got notice last night that a representative from the Zoo is planning to propose a petition that restricts use of fireworks on the beaches. Not that we're expecting trouble, but . . . it's best to stay informed. You all have been very busy, it seems." With a meaningful glance at Sunlit, he added, "And there is nothing wrong with that."

Sunlit gulped.

Slowly they began to move back down the pier, Ebb and Rei still exchanging some pleasantries. Joy had her nose in the air, perhaps sensing whatever Arietta had whipped up that morning. Sunlit's head was spinning. Someone from the Zoo board would be at the meeting? With a safety proposal?

It's a good idea, she thought. *A very good one.* And that made it more imperative than ever that she show up, too.

Just before they got to the gate, Officer Ebb stopped and turned to Sunlit. "Looks like Marine Sanctuary is popular this morning."

Sunlit looked up, expecting to see a crowd of people in porpoise hats. Instead, there was a string of lifeguards approaching the Sanctuary's side door, and each one was carrying a heavy burden of boxes, parcels, or even something that looked rather like an enormous canvas cake.

She couldn't see a lifeguard uniform without thinking of Ige. She scanned the line again and found him—he'd detached from the others and was coming up to the gate, a long-suffering look upon his face.

"The post office didn't want to hold on to your delivery," he informed Sunlit. "And neither do we."

"*My* delivery?" Sunlit repeated, aghast. She watched the lifeguards begin to pile things on the Sanctuary bench, her surprise only growing.

Ige's mouth twitched into a smile. "I have a feeling you'd better tell Pa that you need a bigger emergency barrel."

22

An Important Choice

> *When buying equipment, one must always be careful to prioritize. Focus on the products that will do the most good for the most animals given the amount of money spent. New conveniences are on the market every day, but life-saving supplies are unlikely to simply fall into one's lap; they must be planned out carefully . . .*
>
> —*from* Standard Practices for a Safe & Sanitary Animal Medic

While Joy hung out on the pier chatting with porpoise enthusiasts, Sunlit sequestered herself in the Sanctuary . . . surrounded by boxes.

Her head had caught up with her situation: she'd had a moment to think during Joy's morning swim—a moment during which Ige had helped her move the boxes inside, and had even sent a trainee running to the cafe for refreshments for everyone. Now, Sunlit had an iced tea on the counter and some blissful silence. What she didn't have was a plan, because organization was impossible. There were too many parcels. All she could do was open the nearest one and start to make sense of it all.

First was a sturdy wooden box nailed shut. With careful use of her pen knife, Sunlit managed to work the lid free and discover . . .

Potions! So many new potions, in rows arranged by color: deep blue, shining white, glowing orange and gold. Unlike the strange yellow potion still waiting on the back shelf, Sunlit recognized these. She'd used them almost daily during her university life: cleaning potions, antiseptic potions, and temporary pain relief.

Just seeing so many nestled among shredded paper strands was enough to make her giddy, and she was tempted to stop right there and start organizing them on her exam room shelves. But she couldn't get to her exam room because of a stack of lighter boxes, so those had to come first.

Flares. Half a dozen small boxes contained sets of emergency flares, a new variety she'd never seen even in her university days. The label proudly proclaimed they were totally safe for animals and people, soundless, and ashless. It would have been too good to be true had they come from any other source. But Sunlit was catching on now, and she had a feeling she could trust her benefactor in this case.

Next she moved on to the large cake-like object. It was wrapped in brown paper and tied up so meticulously that she had to resort to cutting strings—and then yet more strings— and every time she thought she was done, another seemed to be snagged on a corner. When at last she got the wrapping off, she still could not make sense of the object, which was squished up in layers . . . until she found one last string and pulled on it.

Then, Sunlit found herself with an inflatable boat shipwrecked on a pile of flare boxes.

"Oh my goodness," she whispered.

Biscuit flew down from the attic and squawked.

"Biz," Sunlit said, unable to contain herself, "we have a boat! An actual boat!"

"*Sailors delight,*" Biscuit replied.

Sunlit laughed and began hunting along the boat's sides, looking for the string which—she hoped—would collapse the craft once more. If she couldn't find it, maybe she'd have Ige take a look at it. But the whole boat was so light and yet so sturdy—it was so easy to manage by herself. When she found a patch on the bottom proclaiming *Teegle's Rescue Craft for Solo Missions,* she had to laugh. It was, indeed, everything it claimed to be.

Eventually she found the string and sighed a breath of relief when the boat collapsed again. In its "portable" form it was still basically the size of Arietta but square—perhaps not *entirely* suitable for carrying about on one's person—but Sunlit could deal with that logistical issue later. She tucked the boat up on the counter and turned to the rest of the mess.

It was fun now. She approached the lopsided parcels, excited to see what they might hold. Each, it turned out, was a canvas shipping bag containing a spell-casting kit with all the herbs, talismans, candles, and other bits or bobs one might need to imbue something with magic. To use them, she'd have to take them to Tanja and perhaps pay a fee for the magic involved, but even that couldn't dampen her excitement. One was labeled as a *never-leak, never-sink* spell that would perfectly enhance the little inflatable craft. Another was *guaranteed to turn any container into a bottomless bag.*

Sunlit knelt beside the pile, tears welling up in her eyes. Her old mentor had thought of everything. Everything was going to be perfect.

Just then a knock sounded at the front door, and Rachel opened the door, letting herself in. "Oh—is this a bad time?"

"No." Sunlit wiped her face, hastily standing up. "No, I was just—um—"

That was when she noticed that Rachel, too, had a large parcel.

"*Love letters!*" squawked Biscuit.

"Biz, hush," Sunlit said, spurred back into words. "Don't mind him, he thinks he's funny. Um—you have something for us?"

"Just if you want it." Rachel sounded a little more bashful than usual. "I ran into one of the lifeguards at the cafe, and they said you'd gotten a new emergency kit, and—well, I didn't realize how *much* of one you'd gotten," she confessed, looking around.

"I'm still going through it," Sunlit said. "I haven't been able to find any kind of rhyme or reason to it yet."

"There's a letter, here. Maybe that's what he meant." Trust Rachel to spy the piece of paper secured to the top of a box—and to be forgiving about Biscuit. She wiggled the envelope free and passed it across a line of other packages, for Sunlit to take. As Sunlit stowed it in her back pocket, Rachel went on. "Anyway, it got me thinking. We did a workshop on emergencies last year, after the big storm, maybe you remember? And we talked at the time about how it's not just having the stuff, it's also having a good plan. So I had this chalkboard just collecting dust ever since I did my spring cleaning and redecorating, and it's way too big for any of my wall space, but I thought if you hung it behind your counter maybe, or in your exam room . . . ?"

Sunlit looked again at the parcel, which was indeed a wide, thin rectangle. It was too big to fit on the wall over the sinks behind the counter without covering up the old maps. Sunlit found she rather liked the maps. But she also liked the idea of having a planning board in her exam room, which was a more private space.

"I know you and Joy just kind of remember everything," Rachel went on. "But just in case, maybe. You could list what patients you have, what they need, things like that."

"It's a great idea," Sunlit said. "We should definitely be doing that. Thank you."

For a moment, the two were quiet. Sunlit recognized now by Rachel's manner that the chalkboard wasn't just a new decoration for the Sanctuary: it was a sort of peace offering. But she didn't recall anything that Rachel had done wrong.

"I hope you'll be at the meeting," Rachel said. "I will be. I'm, ah, helping the Zoo with their petition. And—Taiwo told me about the editorial, how it was from them. I'm—I just wanted to say that I really had no idea."

"I know," Sunlit said, though to her, her voice sounded far away. "I know you wouldn't have wanted anything like that to happen."

Rachel nodded. "And—I just hope you don't think I'm picking the Zoo over you."

Over *you*. Not over the Sanctuary. Something flared in Sunlit's chest. "Of course not, why wouldn't you help them too? You've always been a big help here, I mean."

"I'd like to keep helping," Rachel said, peering through the dim light. "Maybe I could even help keep you in touch with the Zoo."

Sunlit couldn't keep herself from asking the question. Or half of it, at least. "So—you and Mouse—?"

Again, Rachel nodded. "I hope so, at least."

"I'm sure he does too." Sunlit remembered how eager and helpful Mouse had been at the meeting, and sighed. Together, Rachel and Mouse would no doubt be a force for a lot of good. And more than that—they'd be happy. "Yeah, I—I hear what you're saying. I think it's all . . . a good idea."

The way Rachel's face lit up wasn't as exciting as unwrapping the components of the new emergency kit. But Sunlit did find peace in it, and managed to smile faintly back. In that moment, she had a feeling of moving forward—even if they happened to be moving in slightly different ways.

"I have to get back to the shop," Rachel said. "I'll just leave this here against the tanks. It still has the anchors and everything to hang it, too. I hope it serves you well. Thanks so much for understanding, Sunlit, and—I'm really happy for you. You're going to be really impressive at the meeting tonight. With all this preparation, how could you not be?"

How could she not be, indeed? If only she could demonstrate her inflatable boat to the council, instead of actually having to *talk*.

As the door swung closed behind Rachel, Sunlit found herself in a more sober mood. The Sanctuary was unusually quiet (especially now that there was no longer an imp in the corner clicking beads against glass). Nevertheless, she kept going. She pulled the letter out of her pocket and began to read, if only for something to do.

Haven:

Favorable winds this year—the expected bout of migratory flu never came. All the sickness passed us by. The patients' health is your gain. The spring budget had too much left over and I needed to find a reason to spend it. Hope you don't mind!

I know you only asked for a few things, but I trust you could always use another boat. There should be a reducing-weight spell in there somewhere too. And the flares come highly recommended from the alchemy department. I envy you the pen, myself. Let me know how it goes when you test it out.

Find also stores of powdered food and the towels you asked for. What were you going to do with one towel? I'm including a dozen. We've got the money to spend now, and we might not have it later. You know how these things go.

There's some filters and bottles in there too—those are leftover from the exploration expedition. Will tell you about that debacle in person. If I've recovered by then.

Please note that accepting all this is contingent upon you incorporating emergency kits into your presentation on practical sanctuary maintenance at the end of the summer semester. Which will be in person, on campus, just after Litha. Put it on your calendar now.

Hope you like it.

This should all be shipped in a container, by the way. I ordered one expressly. If it doesn't arrive, I'll have to have a word with the university mail room. Again.

Lina

What in Beyond was this *pen* her professor had written about? Sunlit put the letter down on a nearby box and peered around. None of the packages left was as big as the boat had been. But there *was* something large and oblong over by the side door . . .

She stepped over to it carefully and pulled at the wrapping, curious. Out fell four metal poles painted yellow, and then four painted blue, and four painted purple. When she tried to pick one up to make sense of it, it got longer rather than leaving the floor.

Sunlit dropped it immediately, surprised. With a little more rummaging, she found a paper booklet of instructions. *Incredible Open Sea Pen!* it proclaimed. *Guaranteed water safe— fill it up and then nothing gets through! Expands to fit any need! Reusable!*

Overwhelmed with the possibilities, Sunlit sat down hard on the nearest object, which turned out to be a suspiciously squishy box. Ignoring that particular question for now, she made her way back to Professor Lina's letter and read it again. This time the pen comment made sense. And when she reread the last part about the mail room, Sunlit grinned, if only to herself.

She glanced around the mess once more. It certainly hadn't arrived in a container, and she was almost scared to think that more might be on its way. But it was far, far too much to give up. She knew her professor had said that just to needle her.

And somewhere inside, no matter how much she'd dreaded it, she'd known all along that Professor McAlpin would convince her to give a lecture. Academics could be incredibly persuasive—particularly when it came to getting someone else to run their class for a day.

"We have a lot of work to do, Biscuit," Sunlit said faintly.

She looked again at the front door, as though she might see a hole where Rachel had left. But she didn't. She only saw the chalkboard, and the health of her Sanctuary, of all the animals in and around Seaside. She saw, however faintly, opportunity.

"*Cheese and crackers!*" Biscuit screeched from his corner.

Sunlit chuckled. "It *is* time for lunch soon. Let me get these straightened up, and then we'll find something to eat. And . . ."

And then, she decided, she *would* prepare for the meeting tonight.

It might not be as easy or as fun as unwrapping gifted supplies, but it was no less vital. And—the more she thought about it—the more she realized that she did, in fact, have a lot to say.

23

A Heartfelt Plea

> *Most dragons are great folks when you get to know them. But every once in a while there's that one that's going to insist on a legendary battle, like in the old days. Going to face a dragon is a feeling you never forget . . . like your insides are a volcano about to erupt.*
> —*from* I'm An Adventurer Here Myself

Seaside's town hall building had been built specifically to house the town council—an oddity in a town full of buildings made from repurposed ships, docks, and even bait shops. But it still had the feeling of creatively *making do*, because it had been built over a hundred years previously and the town council had grown a little since those times.

Like most of the buildings on Main Street, the town hall was made of wood. It had a high, arched roof standing a story above most of the other two-story shops and apartments, and wide, many-paneled windows flanking the front steps. Though most of the building's exterior was painted white, Across the front of the first story there was a mural depicting the ocean: ships on the waves, and creatures beneath them. Every year, schoolchildren added to the mural during the anniversary of the town's founding. Sunlit didn't often pass it; she was so used to walking along the boardwalk and then cutting through town, most often to get to the post office. But now she lingered in front of the double doors, taking in a giant orange octopus that seemed to be winking at her. It was a reassuring reminder that the town's life and livelihood came from the sea, and most townsfolk did care about Marine Sanctuary's mission.

Inside, a little foyer with a secretary's desk opened up into the grand hall where meetings were held. The room had been designed to be both inviting and respectable. It was two stories tall and circular, with a sunken floor much like an amphitheater. There were no windows, but more murals along the walls depicting scenes from the town's history. A clearly enchanted chandelier gave off light that matched the sunlight outside, while lamps around the periphery provided enough light to pick one's way through the movable benches and chairs.

At an average town council meeting, according to Taiwo, the room was largely empty save for a ring of perhaps a dozen seats at the central, lowest point of the floor. For this special meeting, however, the room was packed. It was a good thing Joy was right behind Sunlit, preventing her from flight.

Instead she had no choice but to scan the crowd. It took only a moment to locate Chip, Pa, Ige, and Fish, who was standing on a stool to wave at them. The group was sitting in a row toward the back along an aisle, which made it very easy for Sunlit to find a seat behind them—and Joy to take the space she needed in the back row.

Pa was on the aisle, with Fish next to him, right in front of Sunlit. As she took her seat beside Joy, she noticed Ige and Chip casually holding hands, and the sight encouraged her. This wasn't just a place of debates and potential public shaming. It was a place for affection, too.

"Did you see the muriel?" Fish asked, turning precariously on his stool to talk to her.

"We did see the mural," Sunlit said, managing a smile. "Is your class going to paint something on it too?"

"Teacher says we could add a school of fish!" said Fish, accepting Pa's stabilizing arm as a matter of course. "But we have to pick what kind."

"I bet you'll be a lot of help with that," Sunlit told him.

Chip turned too, reaching up to poke Fish, who giggled. "Fish knows more kinds of fish than the rest of us put together!"

"Nevertheless, he could talk about them while sitting down," Ige said, leaning over Chip. This was accepted as generally true and as the situation was remedied, Ige turned a knowing look to Sunlit. "Ready?"

"No," she admitted. "But I guess I am kind of curious to see what happens."

"What happens will be overwhelming support for the Sanctuary," Joy put in. "I've been talking it up to all the porpoise people all day."

"No wonder there's so many people here," Chip remarked over his shoulder.

And, Sunlit realized, not a few porpoise hats, as well. And—many of them seemed to be rainbow-colored and decorated with sparkles.

Just then Taiwo took the center stage, looking as put-together as ever in a brilliant purple maxi dress. They put one hand up, whistled for attention, and immediately the room fell silent.

"Welcome, everybody," Taiwo said with a bright smile. "Thank you for coming out tonight. There'll be a special treat for those who stay until the end.

"Most of you know me, but for those who don't, I'm Taiyewo Afolayan Rise—call me Taiwo—and I'm the one who called you here! Every once in a while we on town council see something going on in town that needs to be addressed as soon as possible, and that's why we have these special meetings.

"You probably know what I'm talking about, too, but bear with me so we're all on the same page. Last week in Last Stop, there was a maritime accident and several porpoises were injured. Sunlit Haven from Marine Sanctuary is handling their care, but in the meantime, there's been some unrest here in Seaside. Town council recently saw a proposal to redevelop the area around Marine Sanctuary and to expand our tourism activities. There's also been vandalism directed at the Sanctuary, concerns about crowds trying to catch a glimpse of the porpoises, and recently an editorial in the paper which contained personal attacks in the name of town politics."

Sunlit winced. She hadn't realized someone had complained to the town about the crowd on the pier, but it made sense.

"These kinds of actions can lead to a back-and-forth that is petty and vengeful," Taiwo continued strongly, "and they obscure the point. Seaside is not a town that carries out feuds with its neighbors. Seaside is a town that brings its concerns to the council *before* they become feuds, and talks them out *here*, in this room. In this room, everybody can have a voice."

Applause broke out at that. Sunlit could feel the tension

growing.

"And in that spirit," Taiwo said, gazing confidently around the room as they spoke, "we're going to start things off by hearing a new petition from our neighbors, the board of directors at the Seaside Zoo. Please give them your full attention, and bear in mind that neither their petition *nor* the development plan are confirmed yet, and neither do they need to be mutually exclusive. Tonight is about hearing everyone's concerns and visions. On that note, Mouse and Spot, you're welcome to take the stage."

There was some polite applause, which Sunlit joined in automatically. She was distracted: when Mouse and his feline companion rose from their chairs in the front row, she noticed Rachel had been sitting with them, too.

"Hello, all," Mouse began, with a rather bashful head bob. Fortunately there seemed to be a spell in place that amplified the speaking voice of those in the center of the room, because he did not have the same presence and projection that Taiwo did. However, he did hold himself upright and with authority, perhaps practiced in all his performances for children at the Zoo. Sunlit couldn't help but envy him for his calm. "We're very grateful to Taiwo and to the entire town council for hearing us on such short notice, and letting us join in on this special meeting. You see, we at the Zoo have been involved in the accident with the porpoises from almost the beginning, and it's made the board very concerned about marine safety as tourism activities increase. Not that we don't want tourism, of course—we do benefit from that too, don't you know."

There was a chuckle from the audience at this, and Mouse beamed. Though he seemed to have toned down his usual accent and colloquialisms in a sort of "professional speaking voice," he was still very obviously himself. He went on, "We love having visitors at the Zoo, but from the very start, the goal of the Zoo was always animal protection. But you don't have to take it from me—here to talk to you about that is someone very important. Friends, let me introduce you to Spot, the leader of our board of directors."

Someone had brought a chair forward, and in this sat the orange cat—just as though he had been there all along, and everyone had gathered specifically to see *him*. Sunlit wasn't surprised in the least, but she noticed that a lot of the audience seemed to be. Some turned over their shoulders to look at the back of the meeting hall, and when she followed their gaze she saw Officer Ebb standing quietly in the shadows. He nodded gravely, as if to say, *yes, this is part of the plan.* Beside him, Sunlit thought she could make out Officer Emme from Last Stop.

"Greetings," said Spot. He was clearly making no attempt to be heard, but his words were clear nonetheless. In the audience, not even Joy or Fish were moving a muscle. "I'm sure you're wondering about me. I *am*, as my assistant has told you, the representative of the board of Seaside Zoo, and I have been so for many years.

"In the past we thought we had to hide ourselves," Spot explained. "When a group of animals and I set up the Zoo, we thought it best to hide from the world. We were distrustful of humanfolk, and many of us had every right to be. In those early years, many animals came to our zoo because they'd been mistreated, illegally captured, abandoned, or worse.

"If we had had our way then, you wouldn't even know about us now. But as the Zoo grew, we realized that we needed outside help. We had to deal with contractors to build safe homes for our newcomers. We had to establish trade with Last Stop and

Seaside to make sure everyone was fed. Many on the board, myself included, were unhappy with this reality. We still felt that you, our neighbors, could not be trusted with the truth. And we knew many people would not have taken the truth seriously. In order to deal with humanfolk, we had to pretend that there was a human in charge of the Zoo.

"This screen kept us safe for a while, but the Zoo continued to grow. There are always more animals in need of safe homes. Some animals, like the porpoises, are beyond even our ability to care for. We were thrilled to make contact with Marine Sanctuary and Sunlit Haven. When someone later tricked us into believing she had tried to get the Zoo torn down, we were devastated. To protect ourselves, *we* were the ones who wrote that editorial. But we have since learned that we were misled.

"Why do I tell you all this? Because it matters. *Animal safety matters*, and we at the Zoo are the right ones to tell you about it. We—along with Marine Sanctuary—are the ones who know the risks animals face. The accident in Last Stop and the attempted sabotage from Seaside have convinced us that now is the time to come forward. That is why we bring our proposal to you today.

"The porpoises in Last Stop, now at Marine Sanctuary, were injured by a careless fireworks display. We propose a set of restrictions to prevent such wanton destruction. We propose that all fireworks be detonated at least twenty feet above sea level; that none be shot from a boat, but instead from a sturdy dock. We also stipulate that all firework techniques and enhancing spells be rigorously tested in a fire-proof environment weeks before the planned display. We urge for notices of displays to be posted in advance, so that animals with literacy skills can remove themselves from the area if they so choose. We also require those responsible for the fireworks displays, be they Witches, technicians, or town government, be also financially responsible for any damage they cause.

"A porpoise's life was lost," Spot concluded. "And two more were deeply injured. This is not a trivial matter. We ask for your serious consideration and commitment to animal safety, nothing more. Thank you."

Tail in the air, the cat hopped from his seat and made his way back to Rachel and Mouse. He was oblivious of anyone's reaction, but Sunlit was scanning the crowd carefully. Some were on their feet giving Spot a standing ovation. Others looked skeptical or bored. And a few, particularly a clump sitting right across from the Zoo contingent in the front row, looked downright angry.

"Paper copies of the petition are available for town council members and those who are interested in the details," Taiwo said, sweeping back into the center of attention. "The petition itself will be voted on at our next regular meeting. We have one other presenter who has requested to speak before we open up the floor to the audience."

Chip and Ige looked over their shoulders at Sunlit, but she was bewildered. She'd psyched herself up to talk, certainly, obsessed over all the points she could make and how she might say them, but she didn't remember actually asking Taiwo for an official introduction. And Taiwo wouldn't just volunteer her like that. Would they?

"Our next presenter has also recently submitted a proposal to town council," Taiwo continued. "Their proposal details a new boardwalk enhancement construction project and a program of tourist events, and it stipulates major updates to many parts of the landscape along the beach, including the pier currently owned by Marine Sanctuary. Here to talk about it in person is the chief developer, Heather del Sol."

Sunlit held her breath as Heather del Sol got up to speak. She had been sitting with the angry crowd.

She was also entirely unlike the image Sunlit had had in her mind. Heather del Sol was short and muscular and she walked with a step that screamed *competence,* but she also looked like she might have just stepped off the boardwalk. She was wearing a loose white top decorated with blue flowers and tight shorts over strappy sandals, and her hair was pulled back in twin braids. It was also rainbow-colored, with strands of every hue. Her skin was pink—much like Sunlit's hair, but even darker, a bright color rather than a pastel one. She seemed to have some fairy heritage, if the way she skimmed across the stage was any indication.

"I'll be brief," she said, turning slowly on point to look at the crowd. Like Taiwo's, her voice carried naturally. "I know there's a lot of people who want to talk tonight. And time is precious. But so is our beach, and so is every single business there. This isn't just about Marine Sanctuary or whatever patients they may have. Of course everyone feels awful for the porpoises—who wouldn't? But even though we want all animals to be safe, this town is for *everyone.* And we're all trying to build something better. In order to do that, sometimes we have to physically build something new. That time has come. If we don't build now, Seaside will be left in the dust. By then the porpoises will be long gone and all talk over fireworks will be over. All we'll have left is dreams of what might have been."

24

A New Stand

Sometimes, in the natural course of events, it is necessary to deal with local politics. Animal welfare can attract a lot of interest, but it also needs careful guarding. One must always be professional and poised when dealing with politicians. Remember, the impression you make is the impression your organization makes.

—*from* Standard Practices for a Safe & Sanitary Animal Medic

Dreams of what might have been.

The phrase echoed through Sunlit's mind, even as she tried to pay attention to other speakers. She remembered Heather's name being connected with big dream projects—with the new marina, in fact, which Officer Ebb had said was so well-designed. It was strange to think now that Heather's dream of Seaside might not include space for the Sanctuary. To Sunlit,

Marine Sanctuary was a dream come true.

And that was just another reason she needed to speak. But she wasn't entirely sure what the process was. She'd missed any instructions, deep in her musings. People were lining up and Taiwo was directing them with the calm efficiency of a pilot in a marina. One by one, other speakers were taking their turn.

There were so many. Everybody in the audience, it seemed, had something to say. Sunlit flushed with embarrassment when a whole string of porpoise-lovers got up to sing the praises of a Sanctuary they'd barely seen. But they weren't the only ones who felt strongly. Maryanna, the fishing captain from the marina, got up to speak about her small business and how she needed all the help she could get. And many people got up saying that they owned businesses along the boardwalk and were concerned about losing tourism to Last Stop. Even Coral from the consignment store spoke on the subject, and Sunlit could have sworn she was looking right through her. They'd never quite patched things up after the rumors about Fish last spring. The evening wore on, later and later, past Fish's bedtime—even past her own bedtime. But Sunlit was still in her seat. She'd worked all day to prepare but there never seemed to be the right moment to speak.

And then the next person to stand up was Rei.

He'd been sitting in the row behind Taiwo, and he didn't hurry to take the stage. But no one cut in front of him. Sunlit had noticed it before, and she noticed it now: Seaside paid attention to the Rise family. Even when Rei wasn't trying to steal the show. He'd seemed so normal and relatable to her in person: she wondered how he handled all that scrutiny, day after day.

"Good evening, everyone," he began politely. In his tailored suit he looked far more civilized than he had that morning, but his purple accessories matched Taiwo's dress perfectly, reminding Sunlit that he, just like everyone else here, had a life and loves outside of this room. "My name is Rei Afolayan Rise, and I know most of you may be familiar with my family's business, Rise Enterprises. We have had the honor of working with both Seaside Zoo and Miss del Sol in the past, and to the best of my knowledge, both were admirable partners."

He paused, and began pacing, just as he had at the Zoo. Sunlit's nerves stilled. She had no idea what he was going to say, but she had faith in Rei's brand of diplomacy.

"I have been listening," he said, "very carefully, as you might imagine. My family would be nothing without Seaside. And I have heard, tonight, that many of you feel the same way about your own businesses. But those two things are not quite the same, are they?"

He smiled briefly at the crowd, which was silent, trying to puzzle out what he might say just as Sunlit was. Rei went on, "I have been very fortunate. I inherited my position and a great deal of security. Along with that, I inherited a sense of responsibility, one I think many of you share. Because Rise Enterprises is far-reaching, so is the responsibility I feel.

"The duty I inherited is not just to the family business but to *Seaside*, the town. A town that includes all kinds of people, including animals. A town of tourism and trade, but also where we all live, day to day. Each moment makes up our past, present, and future, just like each resident makes up the town.

"I am concerned with the future of my business, but I also believe that the health of the town and everyone in it are *necessary* to my business. Injuries, accidents, and miscommunications are bad for trade, they're bad for tourism, and they're just *bad*, as I think we can all agree. And the truth is that though it was the porpoises who were injured in this case, *anyone* could fall victim to a wayward spell in the same way. Without safety, what point is there in prosperity?

"For my part, I believe the proposal set forth by the Zoo sounds like an overdue and conscientious starting point. But Miss del Sol's proposal is a starting point, too. Why not talk about how we can make things better *and* safer for all involved? Though we may not end up rebuilding our boardwalk, we can work together to address each business's concerns individually and seek to balance them out. Because Seaside is home to many very unique businesses—Marine Sanctuary included."

Rei looked up, right at her, and Sunlit felt herself stand up without any thought. She was halfway down the aisle before she noticed her heart pounding. But if Mouse and Rei and all the others could talk so openly, then so would she.

"Hello, all," Sunlit said, looking around and realizing she was alone on stage. She saw Taiwo, Clementina, even Ombo from the seal incident, and knew she was officially addressing town council as well as the town itself. Nervously she pulled her hat from her head, and she could feel the curious, interested stares. Even people who had been to the Sanctuary had rarely seen her like this. "I—I'm Sunlit Haven, and like Rei said—or, I suppose, hinted at—I run Marine Sanctuary.

"I didn't want to at first," she said abruptly, because it was true. "And even after it started, I didn't think of it as a business. Just as a way to help animals. That's all I *really* know about—I can't speak to tourism or anything else.

"But I *would* like to say something," she realized. The crowd was a blur of color and the lamplight felt like magic. "Spot talked earlier about how animals need safe homes. I agree with him, obviously, but like Rei said, I think it's more than that. People need safe homes too, and—and for me sometimes Seaside hasn't felt that way. I'm new here, or at least I still feel that way, and—in the past few days, there's been some—some awful things said about me. That I'm not responsible to care for the animals, or that I hate progress and anything fun. It's made me feel like I don't belong, and that scares me, because I don't know what would happen to the animals in the Sanctuary if I was gone."

Sunlit paused, because her throat hurt and there was a tear threatening the corner of her eye. There was a rustle in the room, but as she had her hand pressed against her face, she didn't notice it. "I guess I don't know if it matters, all that stuff about me," she said when she looked up again. "But—but the animals we look after at Marine Sanctuary *are* from here. Most of them were born and grew up here, like Zila and Rainbow, the porpoises. And I think we *do* have a responsibility to look after them. It's not their fault they were hurt, and they can't fix it themselves. So, yes, the Sanctuary gets money from the town—and maybe yes, the people at Last Stop could pitch in, too. And as for the pier," she said, gaining steam—even swinging around to face Heather and Clementina, "I thought we fixed it up really nice. It was half fallen into the ocean when I bought it, and everyone's made it into something we can use. And maybe I *should* close it to the public more often, but the truth is what happened with Clementina was just a random accident and we didn't mean anything by it, not me or Fish or Zila either. It's on the beach and maybe it's not used for fishing, but it is still a working pier for us. We do real work at the Sanctuary, and I'm so proud of everyone there. And I don't care if the town wants to build or have fireworks or not—as long as nobody gets hurt—I just want to make sure that my patients can recover and go on to lead happy lives, because that's what I came here to do!"

By the end of it, she was shouting—because the room had erupted into applause.

It seemed like everyone was standing, Taiwo, Rei, Rachel and Mouse. Sunlit even glimpsed Arietta's blue hair and Officer Ebb's quiet smile. Joy raced down the aisle and onto the stage to curve around Sunlit, bouncing excitedly in place. Fish was right behind her, and he ran straight into Sunlit's legs, wrapping his little arms around her tightly. Sunlit put her hand on his head, grateful, but kept her focus. Clementina had stood up.

She'd been sitting right next to Heather del Sol, and she looked every bit as displeased as she had on the pier. Sunlit wondered if everything, all this turmoil, had come from just that one moment. Even if it had, she was prepared to stand by what she'd said. She just couldn't imagine what Clementina would do next.

"If all that was true," said the councilperson with a sniff, "you should have just said so in the first place."

Sunlit gaped. "You never gave me the chance!"

"It's hard to talk when people are yelling," Joy added loyally.

"In any case," said Clementina, royally, "you're saying it now, I suppose."

"And that's enough said about personal matters," Taiwo cut in, silencing and redirecting the crowd effortlessly. They smiled slyly at Sunlit before going on, "And it's getting very late. If anyone else has something they'd like the town council to hear, find a council person before our next meeting, which will be on the night of the new moon. But before you all go—

there is one more person here who's requested a special chance to speak.

"Oh, no you don't," Taiwo added, as Sunlit tried to shuffle Joy and Fish off of the stage with her. "You three stay right there, you're going to want to hear this special."

Sunlit looked around, confused. No one in the front rows stood up. Instead, from the back of the room, Officer Emme descended.

The officer smiled at Sunlit and her little retinue before addressing the crowd. "My thanks to Taiwo for indulging a last-minute request. Folks, my name is Officer Emme, and I'm here from Last Stop mostly to escort our friends at the Zoo. But also, very importantly, to offer the town's sincerest apologies for the accident and its aftermath." As she said it, she turned to Sunlit. "No one wanted that outcome, believe me, and we're going to be considering the Zoo's fireworks proposal very carefully too. It's the least we can do, given the situation.

"And I'm glad to say that in Last Stop, we also have been thinking hard about our responsibilities," she went on. "Taking on the care of two injured porpoises is no mean feat—as the Zoo directors have informed us. And now that we know about Marine Sanctuary, you can bet we'll be sending more patients to you, one way or another. On which note . . ."

Officer Emme turned back to Sunlit, and this time she was grinning fully. "Maybe down the line you should think about negotiating with Last Stop's town council for ongoing support, like the town council here in Seaside gives. It's only fair. But for now, how would you feel about taking an old fire truck as a thank-you donation?"

Sunlit's jaw dropped. For as much as she had coveted that old magitech vehicle, she had never imagined it would be offered to her. No words sprang to mind, but everyone was looking at her, so eventually she managed, "You—are you serious?"

"Completely," Emme assured her. "I can deliver it tomorrow, if you like. Personally, I say you ought to ask for even more. You're doing the town another favor, frankly."

"But where could we—are we allowed to—" Sunlit turned to Taiwo, who was still standing at the edge of the little stage. Officer Ebb had joined them and was smiling too.

Taiwo grinned. "Last Stop actually reached out to us about it this morning, and so far, everyone I've spoken to thinks it's an excellent idea. But technically, you don't need our approval, Sunlit, since it would be going to the Sanctuary. Although you *will* need a place to park it . . ."

"Somewhere Ige can tinker with it!" called a faint voice that sounded suspiciously like Chip's.

"Perhaps," said Rei from the second row, "we could offer you a garage outside of town? With the understanding, of course . . ."

He was setting up Taiwo, and Taiwo was not one to miss a beat. "On the understanding that you'd take part in the founding day parade!"

Is this real? Sunlit had never had such a strange dream before . . .

"Sunlit," Fish interrupted, looking up at her with wide eyes, "are you really going to have a *truck*? With water in it? Can I ride it? Will you take Zila and Rainbow back to see the Zoo?"

Sunlit pulled herself together, and laughed. If she was going to add a mobile water tank and rescue vehicle to her Sanctuary, the least she could do was drive it through town once a year, and give Fish the occasional ride besides. Now at least she wouldn't have to worry about all those emergency supplies and how to carry them around! But that did bring up one important question.

"Since you said we're doing you a favor," she said, to Officer Emme, "does that mean we can ask for one condition?"

"Sure," said the officer, still smiling. "Shoot."

"Would you teach me and—and a back up person—how to drive?"

There was something like a strangled whoop from the back of the room.

Officer Emme was clearly amused. "I can teach you and your friend Chip to drive, no problem."

Sunlit glanced over her shoulder at Joy, who nodded encouragingly. "In that case, we'd be happy to accept it. *Really* happy. Thank you!"

To her surprise, Officer Emme stepped forward and shook her hand. "We're the ones who should be thanking you, believe me," she said, with feeling. And in a lower voice, she added, "You keep doing exactly what you're doing, alright? The whole coastline's better off with you here."

Sunlit blinked back tears, hardly able to respond when Taiwo stepped in and added, "I couldn't have said it better myself."

25

A True Honor

The giraffe fish is remarkable not only for its long, yellow and brown-spotted fins, but for its gregarious nature. Giraffe fish will routinely make friends with other species—even species who could potentially pose a danger to it. How the species has survived is up for some debate; some say it is this quality which allows the flashy fish to thrive. It does make the giraffe fish an excellent candidate for domestic fish tanks.
    —from Traverse's Guide to Marine Vertebrates, Invertebrates, and Magical Outliers

The next morning found Sunlit reveling in the quiet. Joy was off for a swim, Fish was in school, her friends at work. The noise from the beach and even the crowd at the end of the pier faded easily into the background. The Sanctuary had more visitors than ever, and she knew she'd have to go talk to them soon.

But it wasn't time yet. It was still early, and she could spend this time with Zila and Rainbow.

The porpoises who had started all of this.

But as soon as she thought it, she dismissed it. Like she'd said at the meeting, neither Zila nor Rainbow had done anything to purposefully put themselves in harm's way, that day in Last Stop. How could they have known a fireworks spell would go awry?

And—Sunlit could admit it to herself, after hearing everyone speak last night—it wasn't anyone in Last Stop's fault, either.

Normally she was so focused on care and recuperation (of the animals, of course) that she didn't spare a lot of thought for blame. Not consciously, at least. She might worry if some development was her own fault, but that was different, since she usually didn't interact with an animal until it was already in need of care.

But hearing Spot speak with undisguised condemnation had given her much to think about. Looking back over the meeting and the past few days, she could see how she, too, had been feeling resistance and frustration whenever anyone associated with the accident or magic came up—or really, anyone who wasn't part of the Sanctuary. As though somehow everything was *everyone's* fault.

She wasn't sure what to make of that, exactly. But for the moment, she was able to let it go.

"What do you think, Rainbow?" she asked, as the baby porpoise finished her bottle. "Do you want to try magic to get you back to normal?"

Zila, who had taken to skimming through the shallow water in what Sunlit thought of as Rainbow's deck, prodded her back and whistled a descending tone.

Sunlit was so taken aback that she laughed. The sound seemed to convey disapproval. And she couldn't imagine Zila disapproved of Rainbow, so she had to admit that in this case, he was talking to *her*.

He was *talking*—in his own way.

"Normal is the wrong word," Sunlit agreed. "Is that what you're upset about, Zila?"

The porpoise whistled again.

It wasn't as distinct as the feeling Sunlit sometimes got, and she still wasn't sure if he *actually* understood. Maybe it was her tone he reacted to, just like she reacted to his. Thoughtfully, Sunlit said, "I guess neither one of you will ever be back to normal, even if you might look it. I don't even think *I*'ll go back to normal, especially not if I have a big magitech vehicle to think of."

Rainbow wiggled in her lap, and Sunlit set aside the bottle to tickle her tummy. Though the little porpoise still showed little interest in exploring the annex, she did seem more content.

"You'll have to stay here a while longer, anyway," Sunlit told them both. "We'll try to transition you, Rainbow, to eating fish over the summer, but that sort of thing takes time, especially in a Sanctuary environment instead of in open water. Joy could probably help you with that, though."

Zila whistled more cheerfully this time, and came up to nuzzle Rainbow.

"I'm glad you and Joy are friends." Sunlit smiled. "We're really lucky she's able to help with that kind of thing. All your fishing trips, I mean. And the feeding." Of course, that made her think of un-dyeing them again, so that they actually *could* fish. Sunlit sighed, reaching up to adjust her hat. "I think we *will* try the potion. It'll be easy for you, Rainbow, because we can use the tub. For you, Zila, I think we can use the new pen I just got. One of its main purposes is to keep contaminants from coming out or in, and I have to imagine that includes magic. We could also use the fire truck again, but . . ."

As her voice trailed off, Zila lifted his head and whistled questioningly at her.

"I like the idea of doing it here better," Sunlit told him. "That way, I can set it up and you can approach it from the outside, and if you sense anything you don't like . . ."

She let her voice drift again. This idea of trying to let an animal choose its treatment was not one they'd ever talked about at university. It was, she realized, probably Joy's influence. Exacerbated by the Zoo directors, perhaps.

And it wasn't a bad idea in this case, anyway. Though Tanja had been very confident, Sunlit would still be glad of any kind of confirmation that she could get about the potion's safety. Setting it up so Zila could sense it first, rather than plopping him into it with a levitation spell, was just another layer of precaution.

This time when Zila nudged her, it was gentle.

Sunlit glanced down at him. Rainbow was scooching off her lap, perhaps annoyed by all this movement and talk. The idea made her smile again. "We'll just do our best then, shall we?"

Zila trilled.

* * *

Sunlit spent the rest of her morning talking to porpoise enthusiasts. But though they were clustered around the gate, and they *did* ask questions about Rainbow and Zila, Sunlit slowly came to realize that they were actually *Marine Sanctuary* enthusiasts.

"I heard you talk last night," enthused a dwarf with the unmistakable sea air smell of a sailor. "It was so inspiring!"

"We think *all* animals are as cool as porpoises!" chorused a group of off-duty lifeguards.

"I run a magitech repair shop if you need any help with your truck!"

"I have a sick eel at home, is there anything you could do to help it?"

"We just wanted to say we think the way you decorated the pier is amazing!"

"And remember," said a familiar face, Leila, whose children went to school with Fish, "the invitation for an afternoon off sometime still stands!"

Eventually, Sunlit retreated into the Sanctuary—with a basket of muffins that Leila had dropped off—and let Joy take over answering visitors for a while. The friendly otter was a natural at it in a way that Sunlit could only envy.

She set her basket on the counter and began checking the animals in tanks. The little menagerie of safari-themed fish would be staying for another week, and had settled in well. Biscuit was asleep in the corner. The salamander who refused to be let loose grinned at her from atop its rock.

And then the front door opened.

Sunlit looked up, half expecting Arietta or perhaps Ige. Technically, any of the visitors on the pier could have come into the Sanctuary—there was just so much excitement outside, and so many people passing by only to deliver a short message, that everyone seemed to have forgotten that. Sunlit's heart nearly stopped as she recognized the tall, thin figure in the doorway. This wasn't a friend who had been watching the commotion and come over to check on them.

This was Clementina.

"I suppose you *are* open to the public today?" she asked in an arch tone.

Sunlit straightened from where she'd been peering at the salamander, brushing her hands over her loose pants. "Um, of course. Were you—looking for something?"

It seemed highly unlikely. But what else was there to say?

"No, I am not looking for anything." Clementina drew herself up, and then sighed and collapsed a little. She looked smaller, less perfect. "I wanted to—Heather suggested I should—"

She didn't go on immediately, and Sunlit was confused, so she asked, "Heather del Sol?"

Clementina nodded. "Heather and I have been friends for a long time."

Well, thought Sunlit, *that explains the timing of the development plan.* And also . . . it seemed to explain something about Heather, too. *She must have thought she was acting in defense of her friend.*

"Very good friends," Clementina added softly. "She knew me when my husband died."

Sunlit shifted from foot to foot, uncertain what to say.

Fortunately, Clementina seemed to grow at ease in the Sanctuary's dim interior. She kept talking. "My husband loved this place," she said rather wistfully. "Not this bait shop in particular, of course, but you know what I mean. He loved Seaside. He was always talking about what it could be. It was the same with Heather's family—with her mother. She and my husband were cousins."

Though she felt a pang of sympathy for both Heather and Clementina, Sunlit still had no idea how she was supposed to react to this.

"They had so many plans. There were so many things we were supposed to do together . . . And then he died. Right here, in the bay." Clementina stamped her furled parasol on the floor for emphasis.

Sunlit cleared her throat. Clearly, *some* kind of reaction was expected. "I'd never heard that."

"No, you wouldn't have," Clementina agreed. "It was a long time ago. A very long time."

"It's still sad," Sunlit offered. She'd heard somewhere that Clementina was a vampire, so her idea of *a long time ago* might indeed be a very long time. But the feeling was clearly still there. "I'm sure it must be hard to . . ." *To live in Seaside and see the beach.* Suddenly, Sunlit recalled something Ige had said. That Clementina was usually just fine on town council, until the beach came up.

"Yes, well." Clementina looked away, her gaze drifting unseeing over the Sanctuary's maps and charts. "Times change. He used to tell me that, himself."

She coughed, and pulled herself up again, but she no longer seemed as intimidating as she had before. "I owe you an apology. I have not been a welcoming neighbor. I have no trouble with animals or their care, no trouble with you, and yet . . . it is, as you say, difficult. Sometimes more difficult than I let myself realize."

"Joy is always telling me I make things harder when I don't realize how I'm feeling," Sunlit said. Then once she realized exactly *what* she had said, her hand flew to her mouth, and she drew in a breath again to speak—

But slowly, stiffly, Clementina smiled. "Such is the case for all of us. And once we realize how we're feeling, we must take responsibility . . . as Heather told me this morning."

Gratefully, Sunlit relaxed. "Yes, I've heard something like that too. Um—I accept your apology. And like I said last night, Fish and I never meant any harm. It's just that—"

"This is a working pier," Clementina concluded for her, "and the boy is a child. Of course I understand."

"Oh." Sunlit blinked.

"We never had children," Clementina added, lapsing back into thoughtfulness. "But I've always thought it must be good for them to have something to do."

"Oh. Well," Sunlit said carefully, "Fish does really love helping here at the Sanctuary. We all just get a little caught up sometimes."

"I can see that." Clementina's gaze drifted over her shoulder, to the side door, where Joy could be heard laughing with yet more visitors. She then returned her attention to Sunlit. "I hope the sheer number of guests you've had today is an indication to you that Seaside cares for Marine Sanctuary, too."

"Yes," Sunlit conceded, "everyone's been very kind so far."

"And we'll have no more talk of this not being a home for you."

Sunlit cocked her head, surprised. "Well, I—I can't help that I didn't feel welcome."

"Perhaps not. But you've made it your home anyway, haven't you?"

As she saw what Clementina was driving at, Sunlit admitted, "Yes, I think you could say that. I did have a lot of help."

"And I'm sure you will continue to find that you do," Clementina remarked. She turned to the door, but then back to Sunlit, almost as if she'd forgotten the most important thing she'd come to say. "To have a place like this in Seaside," she said, her voice heavy, "is a true honor. It is something . . . he would have loved."

Sunlit could have needled her. *Even without massive fireworks shows?* She could have said. But even though she still felt a little uneasy with Clementina, she understood that this was very meaningful. It was a truce, of sorts. And who knew what might grow from here?

26

A Complete Peace

Though the sunsets, beach, boardwalk, and many excursions make Seaside a delightful place to visit, the true gem of this town is its community. Seaside has long been a place to pride itself on working together and welcoming others. May it continue to be so for even longer into the future!

    —*from* A Guide to Seaside (for the Discerning Tourist)

Officer Emme was as good as her word.

As Sunlit recovered from her . . . *interesting* . . . interview with Clementina, sitting on the bench outside the Sanctuary with Arietta and Joy eating sandwiches, there came a rumbling from Seaside.

At first, they ignored it and kept chatting. Arietta had been at the meeting last night, of course, but she seemed eager to go over every detail and get their impressions. Joy was only too happy to dish as well. Sunlit was just glad there was a lunchtime lull in their visitors.

But then the rumbling drew nearer.

"Do you think it's one of the boats in the marina?" Arietta asked, peering around even though the fishing marina was hidden behind the Sanctuary building.

"It sounds like it's coming from the street," Joy said, her muzzle swiveling as she pinpointed the sound.

Of the three of them, Sunlit was the only one who had seen the old firetruck in action before. But she was too surprised—too excited, even?—for words. Her sandwich dropped in pieces down to the plate in her lap.

Then Officer Emme blew the horn, and got *everyone's* attention.

The magitech truck was somehow even bigger than Sunlit had remembered it. With wide rubber wheels and an unstoppable, chugging brass engine, it made its way onto the wide area of the boardwalk next to the Sanctuary, stopping just before it hit the pier. Its old orange hood was stained and dirty, the glass pane in front of the driver's bench cloudy with age, and yet it was the most glorious thing on wheels that Sunlit had ever seen.

The truck, parked proudly in a place where no vehicle ever came, immediately attracted attention. But most onlookers kept their distance at first. Meanwhile, Officer Emme swung down from the driver's seat, grinning widely. Officer Ebb was not far behind.

"Special delivery," said Emme, coming over to Sunlit. "Did someone ask for a truck?"

"Oh my goodness." Sunlit stood, and it was only Arietta's

quick thinking that saved her sandwich from clattering to the ground. "Thank you so much! I can't believe it, is it really ours?"

"Keys and all," Officer Emme confirmed, holding out a large brass key on a polished ring. "And you'll get your lessons, not to worry. I have to get back to the station today, but what do you say to the day after tomorrow, early morning sharp?"

"Yes," said Sunlit, instantly. "It's perfect. That's perfect. That'll give me time to tell Chip."

"I'll take charge of the truck in the meantime," Officer Ebb offered, with his own small smile. "Emme has shown me the ropes, enough so I can crawl it out of here. I know where the Rises have their garage. I'm afraid we can't let it stay on the boardwalk overnight."

"Of course not," Sunlit agreed. "When the time comes, I can go with you, I just—"

"Don't put yourself to any trouble," Emme said. "We've got it all arranged. You just focus on your porpoises."

"And on loading up the truck with some emergency supplies?" Arietta suggested. She'd seen the cluttered exam room in the Sanctuary.

"An excellent idea," said Ebb, as Sunlit agreed. Joy was sniffing curiously around the machine—as were more and more tourists.

"But speaking of trouble," Sunlit said, pausing as she turned to Officer Emme, "how are you going to get home? I'm sorry you had to come up all this way."

"Don't worry about me," the officer insisted. "I have a little business with the Rises as well—an errand from Last Stop. I'm sure they'll see me home somehow."

Most likely in a balloon, Sunlit thought. But she didn't have any envy to spare for the idea. She was too preoccupied with amazement at the fact that *she had a truck.*

"Speaking of errands," Officer Emme added, as though she'd read Sunlit's mind. She handed Sunlit a rolled-up piece of parchment. In all the excitement, Sunlit hadn't even noticed it yet. "The paperwork for the truck. Officer Ebb probably has some permits he'd like you to sign, too."

"That I do," the officer confirmed. "We have time. Let them celebrate for now. The whole town knows what's going on, anyway—it's not like anyone's going to be caught unaware and make a complaint."

He winked at Sunlit, and for once, one of his jokes didn't fill her with even *more* anxiety. Because she was hardly feeling anxious at all, not in this moment.

"This is amazing," she said, probably not for the first time. "Thank you so much."

"Our pleasure," Officer Emme assured her. "And while I'm here, would you mind if I took a look at the patients?"

"Oh! Oh, of course not." Sunlit immediately waved Emme along with her, moving toward the gate. It was hard to leave the truck behind, but no doubt Joy and Arietta could wrangle that crowd if need be. She let Officer Emme, and then Officer Ebb as well, through the gate.

"Can't help being curious," he said.

Officer Emme laughed at him. "Sometimes the uniform has advantages."

"You could have seen them any time," Sunlit told him as they began walking down the pier. "I know you'd be . . . respectful. It's just, after the way things went the first night . . ."

"I understand," he assured her. "And I knew you were handling it as you thought best. By the way, I thought you'd like to know that your vandals did come from Del Sol. We have evidence, traces on the posters and the smell that Joy noticed on the can—the company keeps most of its storage in an old cavern underground, outside of town. However, the employees in question—and Heather herself—came in this morning and made a full confession. She's offered to pay you damages."

"Damages?" Sunlit's head swam. "We didn't have any lasting damages."

"Distress counts," Officer Emme said helpfully.

"Oh." Sunlit couldn't deny that she'd been distressed. "Clementina came by here, though, and she explained it all. I'm not so worried about it now. Like I said before, I just wanted it to stop."

"Be that as it may," Officer Ebb said, "you might find it's helpful in the future to have a company like Del Sol Development owe you a favor."

As they drew abreast with the annex, Officer Emme whistled, effectively changing the conversation. From the shaded pool, Zila looked up and whistled back. He and Rainbow had been spinning little circles, playing a quiet sort of game.

"Leaps and bounds better than they were the last time I saw them," Emme remarked. "To be honest with you, I wasn't sure the little one'd make it."

"Rainbow has improved a lot," Sunlit agreed, with pride in her voice. "And I have a potion from the Zoo to help them return to their normal color. It takes a little bit of preparation, and I only just got it, so I was planning on trying it tomorrow."

"From the Zoo?" Officer Ebb leaned his elbows on the pier railing, watching the porpoises resume their little game.

"From—" Sunlit realized that here was the last person she hadn't spoken to about the sea witch—the one person everyone had recommended. Would he be the one to contradict what everyone had said, that the potion was safe? "From the sea witch, Clemency, actually. I guess the Zoo reached out to her before they realized I'd take the porpoises here. I had never heard of her, but everyone seemed to think it was okay. Unless—unless you know different?"

Officer Ebb looked back at her at first, surprised. Then he glanced at Emme thoughtfully. "Last time anyone in Seaside had any dealings with Clemency was the Afolayan Rises' wedding a few years back, as far as I know."

Emme nodded. "It's been even longer for Last Stop. There's still rumors all the time, but she keeps a low profile."

Sunlit decided she didn't need to know about the rumors. "Is there any reason to think she'd undermine the porpoises' recovery?"

"None," said Officer Ebb, confidently. "She wasn't too keen on most folks when she left, but she always had a soft spot for marine creatures."

The tension releasing from between Sunlit's shoulder blades was wondrous. "That's a relief," she sighed. "I had no idea, myself, and I didn't want to put them in danger."

"It's clear that you know what you're doing," Officer Emme said, casting an appraising eye over the annex and the Sanctuary beyond it. "And you've got a lot of public buy-in. Have you considered doing visits?"

"Like tours?" Sunlit was startled at first, but admitted, "We did do them at the university, and the main floor of the Sanctuary has always been open. With everything going on in town, it didn't occur to me, but . . . we *are* going to have Rainbow and Zila for a while at least, to make sure Rainbow's fed. And they've both calmed down quite a bit . . ."

Officer Ebb was still watching her, this time with amusement on his face. "You could limit how many people come by. Do one tour a day, perhaps. Charge for it."

"Definitely charge for it," Emme agreed. "Use the extra money to hire an interpreter to do the tours for you, even."

Sunlit turned this idea over in her mind. "It's . . . it's something to think about," she agreed. "I'll have to talk to Joy. But I think it could be okay."

"And if it's not, then change your mind," Ebb told her. "Say 'sorry folks, we've had to adjust to suit the porpoises.' The porpoises come first, isn't that right?"

Sunlit met his eyes and smiled. "That's right."

* * *

That evening, they pulled picnic tables over to the Sanctuary pier and had a celebratory feast.

Arietta brought over more savory pies and cold salads, as well as a basketful of cookies shaped like trucks. How she'd had the time to bake and decorate them, Sunlit couldn't figure. The baker was as cheerful as ever, sitting at one end of the tables and talking to Pa. For his part, Pa had already pulled Sunlit to one side and told her that Ige's tinkering was all well and good, but if she wanted to replace anything on the truck, she should come to him for the carpentry. He'd make sure the new parts were reliable.

Across from Arietta and Pa were Joy and Fish. Joy was stretched out along the pier with her nose at table level, perfect for snatching tasty things as they were passed around. Fish was bouncing up and down in his seat as he told her, repeatedly, about riding the firetruck to the Rises' garage with Officer Ebb and Sunlit. He'd been talking about that the entire walk *back* from the garage, as well.

And the Rises, of course, had come with them. Rei was sitting next to Fish, politely offering details about the truck and the garage and what kind of animals would fit in the tank as they were required of him. Taiwo had been badgering Sunlit about running away too early from the meeting last night to partake in the surprise treat, enchanted donuts from a new shop in town. Fortunately, Taiwo had had the good sense to bring another platter of the donuts for this evening, and was now badgering Ige instead, this time about how he should lend his lifeguard recruits to the new Sanctuary tour program.

Sunlit had mentioned two or three words about the idea in passing earlier, and Taiwo had immediately taken to the scheme.

"Makes you proud, doesn't it?" Chip joined Sunlit where she stood near the railing, watching the table scene.

It did. It made her heart swell, seeing her friends like this. And knowing that Zila and Rainbow were safe right nearby. Sunlit sighed happily. "I can't believe everything we've managed to do."

"Funny what happens when you keep putting one foot in front of the other," Chip agreed lightly. He offered Sunlit a drink, holding his own back and taking a long sip before adding, "And letting your friends help you, of course."

Sunlit chuckled. "You're never going to let up about that, are you?"

"Never," Chip agreed. "This is my revenge on you for not having grown up with Pa."

"What?" Sunlit was playfully aghast. "What are you talking about?"

"Do you have any idea what it's like to grow up in a seafaring community? Everything's 'aye aye matey' this and 'good crews pull together' and 'tight ships weather the storms' that!"

Midway through a drink, Sunlit laughed, covering her mouth to hide the mess. "I did grow up by the ocean, thank you, but not with sailors. I never heard any of that."

"*Raawk! Hoist the mainsail!*" Biscuit put in as he sailed overhead and perched on a lamppost.

"Except from Biz," Sunlit amended.

"I won't even ask where he got it from," Chip said wisely. "My point is, I have to make sure you hear it all now, so you can suffer the way I did."

"Thanks for sharing," Sunlit said wryly.

"No problem. What're best friends for?" Chip grinned. "Welcome to a long legacy of supportive smothering."

"Well," said Sunlit, smiling again at her table of friends, "it's good to be a part of something."

Out in the waves beyond the pier, she thought she saw a large seal head pop up. But when she looked again, it was safe beneath the waves.

27

A Fresh Start

Magical creatures come in all kinds of colors! Some are even every color of the rainbow. They use their beautiful colors to attract friends or even to speak to each other. Did you know colors can have meanings? Next time you're feeling a certain way, try deciding what color it would be!

—*from* The Children's Encyclopedia of Magical Water Creatures

The next day dawned bright and clear. Biscuit was in good spirits, Joy was full of fresh fish and stories, and Sunlit was feeling lighter than she had in ages. All the soreness and resulting stiffness in her hand had eased with time. And on top of that, it was perfect weather for trying a water-based treatment: no rain to interfere, no strong winds to blow the magically-enhanced water into the ocean. Plus, it was such a perfect beach day that most of the visitors to the boardwalk were on the *beach*, not loitering around the Sanctuary's pier.

All this, but Sunlit had to wait to use Clemency's potion. She'd strictly promised Chip, Fish, and Ige.

Truth be told, it was better that she wait for assistance. She'd excavated her new "traveling pen" from the emergency supplies, and it looked like it only needed one person to set it up, but setting it up and then keeping it steady while also coaxing an adult porpoise inside was another matter entirely.

And naturally everyone was very curious to see the results.

Fish was the first one to appear in the Sanctuary that afternoon. He raced through the open front door, his hands out like wings behind him. "Sunlit! Guess what I am!"

Sunlit looked up from where she'd been drawing lines on her new chalkboard, preparing it for all the information it would host. This new evolution of Fish's "marine creature charades" made her smile. "I don't know. A flying manta ray?"

"No!" Fish said, as he ran loops between the tanks and the exam room screen.

"An imp?"

Fish paused to give her a look. "Imps don't have wings."

"True, for water imps," she admitted, chuckling. "Okay. Um, a seagull?"

"I'm a dragon!" Fish cried. "A sea dragon! Rawr!"

"*Rawr!*" agreed Biscuit, flapping his own wings atop his favorite perch.

"Sea dragons come in all kinds of colors! I'm going to be the most colorful one of all!" Fish continued running around the room, nearly careening into Chip and Ige at the door.

Chip smiled apologetically at Sunlit. "Apparently they've been reading myths in school lately. Someone confessed to the teacher that they had caught the imp and brought it into the school bathroom because they wanted to know what magic could do, and this was part of the solution."

"Scaring them stiff with stories of magic gone awry?" Ige asked, an eyebrow raised as he watched Fish.

"Or inspiring them, apparently," Chip replied.

"As long as *our* magic works today, that's what matters," Sunlit said firmly. She did have to agree with Chip, at least privately—Fish didn't seem intimidated in the least. "Are you all ready to get to work?"

One and all, they were. They collected Joy from her napping spot on the pier and gathered at the annex. Ige took over setting up the pen, directing Joy and Chip to help him as they wrangled it to fit perfectly at one end of the sunken boat. Fish abandoned his wings for suckered tentacles, sticking to Sunlit's side like a sea star as she washed out and set up Rainbow's tub. Once both teams were ready, Sunlit looked up.

"Let's do Zila first," she told everyone. "He'll be able to withstand any side effects better, and he'll feel better knowing what might happen to Rainbow, too."

Zila, who was lurking in the middle of the boat, whistled in agreement.

"Since we're not using the entire bottle in one go, do you know the proper amounts?" Ige asked.

Sunlit held up a piece of scribbled-on paper from her shirt pocket, and the potion bottle, which now had taped marks on its side. In this circumstance, preparation and leadership came as naturally to her as breathing. "That was my morning project," she confirmed. "I did the calculations three times."

"Measure thrice, cut once," Chip said, rubbing his hands together. When Ige gave him a reproving look, he added, "metaphorically, at least. Shall we?"

"Okay." Sunlit took a deep breath. She'd thought this over carefully. "Fish, I want you to stay here in the shallows with Rainbow, alright? It's very important that she stays calm. I'm going to go over to the pen." With the tide all the way in, the water in the main section of the boat came up to her chest, as it did Chip. Joy was long enough to rest on the bottom, and Ige was swimming—and making it look effortless, aided by his merfolk tail. Sunlit bobbed toward them and then hauled herself up to sit on the boat's edge so that she could look into the pen. Its sides rose up a few inches above the water—high enough to keep the potion in, but not so high that Zila couldn't get in or out if he wanted to.

"Okay, it's full of water, good," Sunlit said. So far, everything was working exactly as it was supposed to. "Now, Ige and Joy, if you could go underwater and secure the bottom in place—it's supposed to extend from the left side. Chip and I will hold it steady."

Ige and Joy set to work. The sides of the pen were an opalescent mesh, and the bottom was strung to one side like a tent door pulled open. Once it was tied closed, however, the entire pen glowed.

"That's how we know it's activated," said Sunlit, who had read the entire manual cover to cover. Twice. "Anything inside will stay there. Now all we have to do is put in the potion, then get Zila in."

At her side, the porpoise clicked with curiosity.

She smiled at him. "Here goes nothing."

She shuffled to make sure she was secure on the old wood, and then uncorked the potion. Slowly, carefully, she poured the bright yellow liquid in.

"Whoa," Chip said, as the magic quickly spread through the pen. "That is pretty neat."

The potion in the water didn't seem diluted at all—in fact, the entire pen now glowed neon yellow. Fish was straining on his tiptoes to see from the other side of the boat, one hand on Rainbow's back. Sunlit looked down at Zila.

"Okay, you're up," she told him. "I don't know if you can understand me well enough to know that you could jump in. If he doesn't," she added to her companions, "we'll need Joy and Ige to help lift him. But he might get the idea."

"I think he will," Joy said. She swam over so she was next to Zila, her nose at the edge of the pen. Then she rose up and looked over the wall into the yellow water.

Zila bobbed, clicking at her.

"Like this," Joy said. She turned sinuously through the water and swam to the end of the boat, then back to the pen with speed. But she stopped just short of diving in herself. Sunlit was quietly thankful: she had no idea what effect the potion would have on a normally-colored animal. And a *fur*-covered animal, at that.

Zila watched Joy with interest, then turned to Sunlit and whistled.

"Go on," she said, feeling for just an instant foolish before disregarding the sensation. She reached out through the water, slipping off her glove to touch Zila's side. Focusing all her energy on being as encouraging and supportive as she could be, she added, "You can do it. It's okay. This is going to help." With all her heart, she set aside her doubt and just *believed* it.

Zila whistled again. Then he flipped backward through the water, slipping from Sunlit's hand. She lost sight of him for a second and then he reappeared, leaping through the air.

With perfect execution, he dove into the sparkling pen.

There was a bright flash, and the scent of fresh rain filled the air. Sunlit blinked. Zila popped his head out of the water and trilled at her.

He looked exactly as a textbook western bay porpoise would: blue-grey on top, light grey on bottom. There were no scorch marks, no streaks, no sign at all of any magical explosion or injury.

Chip let out a whoop. "The green's all gone!"

"The yellow is receding from the water, too," Ige observed.

"The spell's been used up," Sunlit realized. She felt a rush of appreciation for Clemency, the witch who had so neatly designed her potion.

Joy bobbed up and bumped noses with Zila. "He sure seems pleased about it!"

Indeed, the gray porpoise twirled and leapt again, and did loops around them all as they tested the water, collapsed the pen, and made their way to Fish and Rainbow. Fish was laughing at the way Zila was flicking droplets of water around. Even in the shade, the annex was full of tiny rainbows, it seemed. An effect of the magic? Or simply the relief? Sunlit couldn't tell.

She sat beside Rainbow's tub, this time with a lightened heart. "Okay, baby. Your turn."

Zila sped into the shallows nearby, forcing Chip and Ige to lean back against the ship's rail. Joy lingered in the deeper water. This time, Fish settled next to Sunlit on his knees, watching the potion stream into the tub.

"Whoa," he said, just like Chip, as he watched the water inside turn yellow.

"*Whoa!*" agreed Biscuit, a shadow on the mast above the sail that shaded them.

"Zila did it himself, but we'll definitely have to help Rainbow," Sunlit said, focused on the task at hand. "She doesn't have her strength back yet, not enough to make a leap like that. Fish, can you help direct her? Touch her very gently, like this."

She demonstrated with her palm flat on Fish's arm. Fish nodded; no one in Beyond could have been more serious in that moment. Dutifully, the little boy moved toward the baby porpoise, holding his hands out flat to guide Rainbow's head.

"We'll do it together," Sunlit said, reaching out to put her own hands under Rainbow's belly. On instinct, she did the same thing she'd done with Zila, focusing all her energy on being as supportive as possible. She had no idea if it had worked before, but—but this time, she felt Rainbow wiggle a little, and she heard Zila trill reassuringly.

Together, Sunlit and Fish lifted Rainbow up and into the tub.

There was the same flash and smell as before, this time mingled with Fish's delight as he got to watch the spell up close. Biscuit cawed and flapped above them. And in the aftermath of the spell, there was the same gray skin as the little porpoise lifted its head—just for a moment.

Then Rainbow looked Sunlit right in the eye and a shiver of blue ran down her curved back.

"What?" Chip started forward, Ige right behind him. Zila clicked, uncertain.

"Didn't the potion work?" Joy asked, sitting up on her hind legs to see better.

Sunlit kept her gaze trained on Rainbow. The baby was perfectly gray again. Like nothing had happened. But they hadn't *all* imagined it . . .

"I think it did work," she said slowly. Curious, guided by

instinct once more, she reached out to rest one ungloved finger on Rainbow's head. Like a ripple, a shiver of pink went out from the point of contact.

But when Fish reached out impulsively and placed his palm on the baby's back, there was nothing.

Unable to stand the suspense, Zila lurched up and stuck his snout into the tub as well. For a moment Rainbow shivered with the full spectrum of colors, leaning into her parent, but then she went gray again.

"I think she can do it on purpose," Sunlit murmured. "I think she controls the color. Blue—that's what I was thinking as I lifted her up—calm, gentle, healing."

"Well, we know your touch has a way with animals," Joy commented.

For once, Sunlit didn't bother fighting her on it. "I did the same to Zila, but—but he hadn't been affected as strongly in the first place, maybe. Maybe because of the different effects on Rainbow from the beginning, it was always going to work out this way."

Rainbow nudged at Fish and Sunlit, clearly looking to get out of the tub. Once they'd settled her in the annex at large, she began nosing around Zila, Sunlit, and Joy. Fish followed her, gently stroking her sides from time to time.

"She's looking for food, I expect," said Joy, amused. The baby porpoise had been gray now for some minutes. She looked for all the world like nothing had happened to her at all.

"She gets along much better than she did before, at least," Chip observed.

Ige was watching Sunlit. "Are you worried about her still?"

Sunlit looked up, wonderstruck. "Actually . . . no. I can't explain it, but I really do think she can control it. She'll be fine.

I feel . . . calm."

"You should feel loved," Chip said, flopping down in the water next to her. "She loves you. Look."

Rainbow bumped her head into Sunlit's sleeve, and this time another pink shimmer arced across her smooth skin.

Sunlit grinned down at the baby porpoise. "She's talking in color," she said, still amazed. "I've never heard of anything like it. Except in some jellyfish, and supposedly some dragons, and—"

"And," Joy continued for her, "it's magic."

Sunlit met her eyes with a little laugh. "Okay. You got me. It's magic."

"I'm gonna be a magic porpoise too," Fish decided. "Do you think if I was, I could be friends with the water imp?"

This time, everyone laughed, and Sunlit savored the moment. Rainbow was well. Zila was healthy. They could live their lives in peace. For all the questions that remained and developments that lay ahead, Sunlit knew right now that she and her friends were perfectly fine.

In fact, in the end, all the disturbances and expressions of the past few days had made their little habitat more alive.

More *colorful.*

Epilogue

Two weeks after the porpoises had left the Zoo, Spot was feeling quite pleased with himself. His—or rather, *the Zoo's*—fireworks proposal had been added to town law, with very little change, in both Last Stop and Seaside. The porpoises, by all accounts, had made a full recovery aside from the matter of feeding the baby. And most of all, he had a new newsletter with which to speak to the public.

"This your final draft?" Mouse asked, coming into the round office and finding a typewritten document on the desk.

"You could look it over," Spot conceded, in a voice which both demanded that he *do* look it over, and that he find nothing wrong with it. "Can't be too careful."

Mouse sat down to his work at once. "Want to strike the right tone and all, what?"

"What indeed," agreed the cat. "Since this will be the very first Letter from the Editor for the new Seaside Animals Gazette, I don't have to tell you how important it is."

"You don't have to tell me how long it is, either," said Mouse, sifting through multiple pieces of paper.

Spot stiffened. "There is much to be said!"

"Not if you're Sunlit Haven," Mouse replied cheerfully. "Her 'News from the Beach'" segment was only five hundred words. And that was *after* Rachel made her write more, don't you know."

"Impossible," Spot declared. He knew Sunlit to be a very competent caretaker. She must have *plenty* to say on the subject of marine animal news and rights.

"Nonetheless, there you have it." Mouse slid a pair of wire spectacles on and proceeded to read. This task might have been easier had his glasses' frame not been bent at such odd angles it barely could cling to his head, but he didn't stop to think about that.

Spot could have let his assistant read in silence, of course. But it was a rainy afternoon and the Zoo had been quiet that day, so there wasn't much else to think about. He'd already spent half an hour grooming his tail. So now he strutted proudly back and forth on the desk, enjoying the feeling of the solid wood under his paws.

"We'll have to make sure everyone gets a copy," he said, not to anyone in particular but just to the world, to show it how effective he was. "All the houses in the Zoo will have to carry it. We must be sure we order enough."

"Already put the order in," said Mouse, not adding that the number ordered had been, to him, astronomically high. But, as Rachel had pointed out to him, they did have a month to sell this edition before they planned to publish the next one.

And good thing too, because Mouse wasn't certain he wanted to play "editor of the Editor" more often than once a month.

". . . Send them to Last Stop, and Seaside too," Spot was saying, his little nose in the air. "Though I suppose Rachel and Sunlit will take care of that."

"Mostly Rachel," said Mouse, out of loyalty. "Though Marine Sanctuary will carry them too. They have a specially-built magazine stand and everything."

"Magazines!" Spot's tail fluffed at the indignation of it, but then consoled himself by imagining the rack filled with paper newsletters with his words printed on the front of each one. "To each their own, I suppose. And speaking of—we should send a copy to Clemency."

Mouse, whose hand had been wavering over a nearby pen—wondering if it was worth it to suggest a grammatical change to the Letter—looked up at that. "The sea witch? You think she wants to read about the new penguin routine and updates to the nocturnal house?"

"I was thinking she'd want to read about our efforts to promote good pet care in the summer heat," Spot retorted, "and perhaps the article on the porpoises."

Mouse scratched thoughtfully at his chin. "Did anyone tell her that her potion worked?"

"The newsletter will," said Spot.

"Wouldn't she want something more personal than that? I might, if I'd gone to all the trouble to toss together something like that. That was some high-grade magic, you know."

"I do know, and that's why I asked for it," Spot said archly. "And likewise, Clemency knows her work wouldn't fail. She doesn't need a report from us on that score. However," he added, turning away from his assistant to look out the window at the gray rain, "she might want to know about the Sanctuary where her work went."

Mouse said nothing. But while Spot was distracted, he picked up the pen and made a quick correction. His employer, he told himself, would never notice.

And anyway, what was the harm in a little newsletter?

About the Author

Elle adores ocean life, magic, and above all, found communities. As a historian and educator, she believes in the value of stories as a mirror for complicated realities. She currently lives in New Jersey with a grumpy tortoise and a three-legged cat.

Find more stories of Sunlit and her friends at ellehartford.com. And while you're there, sign up for Elle's newsletter to get bonus material, behind-the-scenes sneak peeks, and terrible jokes!

Also by Elle Hartford

Marine Magic:
   How to Care for Cursed Fish, book 1

The Alchemical Tales series:
   Beauty and the Alchemist, book 1
   Cold as Snow, book 2
   Mermaid for Danger, book 3
   Cry Big Bad Wolf, book 4
   Cinders to Dust, book 5
   Death Pulls the Strings, book 6
   A Thousand and One Alibis, book 7
   Tangled Up in Murder, book 8

Pomegranate Cafe Romance:
   Worthy in Love, book 1
   A Tale of Rowan and Daisy, book 1.5
   Strong in Love, book 2
   Steady in Love, book 3
   Sweet in Love, book 4